GW01425169

The Septillion of Hheserakh

Tracey Norman

a collection of legends from

The Fire-Eyes Chronicles

First published in Great Britain in 2018

by Aamena Press, Devon

Text copyright © Tracey Norman 2018

The right of Tracey Norman to be identified as author

of this work has been asserted by her in accordance with

the Copyrights, Design and Patents Act 1988.

All rights reserved. No part of this publication may be

reproduced, stored in a retrieval system, or transmitted

in any form or by any means, electronic and mechanical,

photocopying, recording or otherwise, without the prior

permission of the author.

ISBN 978-1-9997554-1-6

www.thefireeyeschronicles.co.uk

The Fire-Eyes Chronicles artwork by Avalon Graphics LLC

For MN, whose support is everything

Welcome to the Hheserakhian Empire!

I am the Storyteller and am here to guide you through some of the most well-known of the Empire's legends. You will encounter dragons, standing stones, heroes and cursed artefacts. There will be tragedy, laughter, peril and ingenuity, all of which will, I hope, help to shape your view of the Empire. True, it has its troubles, but it is not alone in that, for the world is an unsettled place.

Many of these legends were told to the famed elf ranger Aamena Hinnorwen as she was growing up in the Great Forest in the far north of the Hheserakhian Empire. Perhaps one day, you may share them with your own children.

You can find out more about the adventures of

Aamena Hinnorwen and her companions at

www.thefireeyeschronicles.co.uk

Table of Contents

The Song of Bál and Máni

In the beginning, the universe was a lonely place of dark and light, of burning heat and searing cold, ruled by two primordial dragons.

Bál, the Obsidian, Ruler of Glorious Light, and his Consort, Máni the Argentate, Queen of Infinite Darkness, guarded their worlds with the utmost care. The Infinite Darkness and the Glorious Light were separated from each other by an immense, yawning chasm filled with molten lava which raged and spat. Bál tended to this Eternal Fire, fanning it gently with his vast wings and creating beautiful patterns and colours for the amusement of his beloved Máni. She watched from afar as he told the story of his love for her through the Fire's exquisite dances. In turn, she stretched out her silver wings, reflecting the light of his Fire, which shimmered across her delicate scales in countless tiny points of light and echoed her love for him.

Yet though they loved each other, Bál and Máni were each obliged to keep to their own worlds, she in the comfort of her velvet blackness and he in the exhilaration of his scorching flame. Their worlds gently rotated, sometimes taking them away from each other for a while, but as each rotation completed, they would find each other again and resume their love story.

But there was a time – a magical, exquisite time – when the lovers could be together. When their worlds were aligned in a particular way, the darkness consumed the light and created the In-Between, a mystical bridge across the chasm which allowed them to step out of their own world and into the other, for a brief moment.

Bál and Máni yearned for the In-Between, that sacred, blessed bridge to pure joy. Whether he came to her world, or she to his, they both thrilled at the presence of their beloved and basked in their fond affections. They danced together and sang sweet songs into the universe, which heard them and rejoiced in their perfect love.

Alas, these happy moments were all too short, for, as the worlds kept turning, the magical time would soon end and the In-Between would vanish. The lovers knew that their time in the other's world was both precious and dangerous. Becoming trapped in the other's world would mean certain death.

So, much as it tore at their hearts to leave, they made certain that they always returned to the In-Between in plenty of time, crossing it carefully from one side to the other, ready to resume their love story and adore each other from afar.

On one such occasion, to their great joy, Máni had produced seven eggs, which Bál carefully rolled into his fire with his claws. The eggs were beautiful, truly the products of a pure and unblemished love. Four were of blackest obsidian, their scales as strong and sure as their parents' hearts, reflecting the firelight back upon itself in an unending circle of dancing flame. Two were of both obsidian and silver, the deep black scales dusted with tiny specks of perfect light which glistened and sparkled in the fire. The seventh egg, however, was very different.

This egg was almost silver-white in colour and its delicate, graceful scales shone with a mystical light. As Bál tenderly cradled it in the fire, the glow from the flames was reflected on every scale, so that the entire nest was bathed in bright, divine radiance. As the tongues of fire licked at its surface and warmed it, the egg seemed to suddenly explode into a dazzling ball of light. It shone brighter than its father's fire, brighter even than its mother's silver brilliance. Bál and Máni gazed at their brood, delighted, knowing that each was destined for greatness – one more so than its siblings.

Their parting on that occasion was more devastating than usual, for Máni knew that she had to leave her children in the care of their father, for only he could reach into the flames they needed to nurture them and ensure their survival. His fire was too much for her and she had been obliged to watch from a distance as he gently committed their children to the life-giving flames, which would protect them until they were ready to hatch. As their time together drew to a close, Máni found it almost impossible to leave. She and Bál sang one last wistful song to the universe, then she set out on the journey across the In-Between, turning back frequently to gaze at her beloved as he watched from the edge of his world of fire.

The journey, already treacherous, was even more so for Máni on this occasion, for her eyes were filled with tears, clouding her vision. She stumbled many times, her usually graceful feet failing her and almost pitching her into the cruel abyss below. Bál, powerless, watched fearfully, scarcely daring to breathe as she slowly made her way across the In-Between.

She was almost across when the In-Between started to shimmer. Bál realised how careless he had been. He had been so caught up in his own selfish joy that he had not ensured that Máni had sufficient time to cross in safety. Now her life was at risk.

In an agony, he watched and waited as she retreated further from him and the In-Between shimmered more strongly as its temporary hold on both worlds weakened. Bál knew that the connection could be lost at any moment. A terrible dread seized his heart as he watched and waited, knowing that there was nothing, nothing at all, that he could do for Máni now.

Máni was so lost in her grief that, at first, she did not notice the In-Between shimmering beneath her feet. It was only when she felt the substance of it change that she dashed away the tears and took in her surroundings. She realised the danger she was in and quickened her pace. The comfort of her dark world lay just ahead, but she could feel the increasing heat from the abyss below as the In-Between's tenuous hold on their worlds began to dissipate, returning everything to its former state. Faster she ran, faster, faster. All the while, the heat swelled around her, blistering her beautiful scales, scarring them with its searing lava kisses.

The In-Between shimmered again, this time more strongly than before. For a brief moment, Máni felt as though she was walking on air, as though the In-Between had simply ceased to exist. She gasped and cried out, but then the surface was once again rough and uneven beneath her feet.

Faster she ran, faster, faster, all the time battling against the increasing pain of the heat from the abyss. And as she ran, she knew Bál was there, watching, desperately willing her to reach the safety of her world.

Suddenly, the In-Between flickered violently and vanished. Máni screamed as she once again felt herself walking on air – but this time, the In-Between did not shimmer back into life. It was gone. The worlds were shifting and she was still caught in the abyss between them. Desperately, she spread her burned and pain-ridden wings, beating them frantically to lift herself away from the heat below. Oh, the pain! It coursed through her body, sending her mind whirling to its darkest corners in an attempt to block it out. She tried to focus on the edge of her world, so close now, and yet still so very far from her.

She could hear Bál's voice, hear the horror in words she couldn't make out as the heat began to consume her. Steeling herself against its cruel bite, she pushed towards her world with every shred of strength remaining to her, but it was not enough. She could see the damage on her scales and wings and knew that she was doomed. Summoning all her strength and courage, she managed to turn back to where Bál was standing on the edge of his world, his face a mask of horror and devastation as he, too, realised that his beloved was lost.

She tried to call out to him to tell him of her love, but the unyielding heat choked her and burned her throat. He was shouting to her, encouraging her to try to get to safety, but she knew it was too late. All she could do was hold out her battered wings and reflect his beautiful Light in a final goodbye. Bál, realising what she was doing, created seven flames, which he fanned into a circle, then placed one large flame in the centre, fanning it until it was white hot. He then stood over the flames as they danced, his wings spread protectively over them. Máni knew it was his final message of love. She was the white flame, surrounded by her seven children, and Bál would protect all of them. Her heart overflowed with love, even in the midst of her agony.

Suddenly, Bál saw his beloved Máni explode into a million shimmering pieces of brilliance as the heat of the abyss finally consumed her. With tears flowing from his eyes, he could only watch as the universe was peppered with sparkling points of white light which illuminated the space all around him. As he watched, the lights hung in the air and he wept anew at the beauty of it, entranced by the patterns they created. For a time, half-blinded by grief, he wandered along the edge of his world, gazing at the lights above.

All at once, he saw a pale glow up ahead, familiar and yet unfamiliar. Puzzled, he approached with some caution, weeping once more when he saw the source of the light.

In front of him, in a gently sloping valley, a scattering of Máni's argentate scales lay on the ground, each casting a soft light that came from within. He found some teeth and claws nearby, illuminated by the glow from her scales. Carefully, Bál gathered everything and returned to the nest, where he tended to the eggs before moving some distance away and laying the scales, claws and teeth out on the ground before him. His eyes wet with tears that would not stop, he caressed the scales, feeing their delicate beauty, their pristine smoothness. Some were damaged and these he set to one side, for the sight of the scarring was too much for his aching heart to bear.

He sat unmoving for some time, wave after wave of grief crashing over him in a torrent of anguish that would not abate. It was only when he noticed another new light in the space above him that curiosity saved him from despair.

There was a strange object high overhead, glowing with the same white light as Máni's scales, yet this was much brighter, almost as bright as the hottest flame, but ice-cold. He stretched out his wings and flew up a little way to see what was creating the light, for it was like nothing he had ever seen before.

The object was almost round and was pitted all over with craters and scars. He realised with shock that this was Máni's heart, ripped from her body and thrown into the space above, where it was now glowing with a familiar silver-white brilliance. In spite of the gouges and the wounds it had suffered, Bál had never seen anything so beautiful. He returned to his world below, gathering up Máni's scales and cradling them in his hands as he had cradled their eggs.

As he sat staring up at Máni's heart, he knew he had to do something to commemorate their love. He tried to tell their story in his usual way, but his heart screamed with the agony of loss and he found himself unable to continue. His hot tears splashed onto the scales in his hands, making them malleable. Bál suddenly had an idea and began fashioning the scales into a sphere. Where his tears fell, strange, new, green life sprang up and bodies of water formed. Máni's scales became more and more malleable and soon Bál had reached deep into his imagination and fashioned countless tiny creatures to populate his new world, each containing a minute part of his lost love and forever tied to her heart, which now shone brightly overhead. Her teeth became rocks, her claws became mountains. Bál added fire to his creation, a core to warm his creatures. Raising the sphere high, he sent it hurtling through the space above towards Máni's heart. As it neared, it slowed and then settled into a graceful arc around the glowing silver orb.

Bál watched its slow, steady progress around Máni's heart, delighted. He would warm his creatures by day with his fire and Máni would light their world by night with her brilliance. He would teach them to love her as he did, so that they could join with him in worshipping her, the most beautiful, gentle mother of all.

Frodleikr's Gift

It is said that the magic mineral frodleikite is created when a dragon dies and its body returns to the earth from whence it came, joining with the fire of its obsidian father and the tears of its argentate mother – for all dragons come from the same line.

The seven children of Bál and his beloved Máni grew up into fine, strong creatures, each with its own distinct colour and personality.

Bál guarded them alone, tending them as they lay curled in their eggs. As they struggled from their shells towards his comforting warmth, he delicately picked the broken shards from their backs and heads with his long claws. As they grew, he held them in his palms so they could practice their first tentative attempts at flying, stretching their tiny wings and snorting clouds of smoke. And every night, he folded his vast wings over them, curling them in the curve of his obsidian tail, where no harm could come to them.

He loved them all, but he knew that each was destined for a very different path.

First, there was the red, the fiery Ofríki, whose iron will dominated his siblings. They endured his tyranny, although they often came to blows, particularly his sister Meinsamr. Her scales were a shining, unblemished obsidian like her father's and she greatly enjoyed watching the patterns made by Bál's flames as they reflected on her flanks and tail. Ofríki's imperious nature conflicted with her own short temper and she would attack him fiercely at the slightest provocation. Her violence, coupled with her sister Hefnd's desire for vengeance at every perceived slight, made them a formidable partnership.

Hefnd's scales were the same brilliant, rich green as the lush foliage on the world her father had created after the death of her mother. She and her brother Flár would often fly up to the world and compare themselves to what they saw around them. Flár was the smallest of the siblings, his scales the same deep blue as the world's oceans. He loved flying close to the surface of the ocean, watching his shadow speed along beneath him. It gave him a sense of power that he never felt in Ofríki's presence, where, in order to establish his authority, he became a false friend to his siblings. If he overheard Hefnd and Meinsamr talking of Ofríki, or found that Meinsamr had jeered at something Hefnd did, he would, straight away, reveal this and then retreat, watching the ensuing fighting with a twisted, satisfied smile.

Bál watched these four with a heavy heart, for he knew that their path to happiness would be fraught with obstacles along its entire length. The only thing which united them was jealousy of their three other siblings.

These three were as different as it was possible to be. There was Jafnadr, whose bronze scales reflected any light with a soft glow. Jafnadr had a strong sense of justice, always ensuring that punishments were doled out as appropriate to those who started arguments or fights. He was closest to his argentate sister Hreysti, who, with no concern for her own safety, would elbow her way between her siblings to prevent or stop a fight.

Every time Bál looked at Hreysti, he saw her mother, his beloved Máni. Yet where Máni had been soft and gentle, Hreysti was feisty and valiant. It was the seventh, however, for whom he had the most affection.

Frodleikr, the golden dragon, whose elegant scales could reflect any light with such brilliance that it hurt to look upon him. Frodleikr the learned, who sought knowledge as a drowning man seeks land and a starving man seeks bread. Like Hefnd and Flár, Frodleikr was fascinated by the world his father had created and spent much of his time there, marvelling at the northern ice caps, the shifting face of the deserts, the ever-changing kaleidoscope of the sea and sky. Often, he would perch atop the highest mountain, watching, as the light of his father's flame faded and made way for the cooling, gentle glow of his mother's silver heart.

Frodleikr was especially fascinated by the tiny creatures his father had made and, knowing that they were created out of Bál's love for his lost Máni, had a special place for them in his heart. As his knowledge of the world grew, he shared what he learned with the tiny creatures, carefully etching the world's secrets onto a set of stone tablets with his long claws. These he presented to the Elders of each of the races, explaining how they were to be used and revered. Nothing gave him greater joy than to see the creatures experimenting with the knowledge he had bestowed upon them, curing their ills and making new discoveries of their own, which they would then delightedly share with him. He, Jafnadr and Hreysti were beloved of the tiny creatures, who welcomed them warmly each time they visited, providing the very best of wine and sustenance and beautiful gifts they had made to demonstrate how their skills were increasing. The three dragons cherished these treasures, carefully carrying them to their nests and setting them out to admire daily.

When Hefnd and Flár saw the love their siblings enjoyed from their father's tiny creations, it stung, for they themselves were not well-loved. They took, rather than gave, damaged rather than protected and scared rather than befriended, so the races feared and mistrusted them. There were no gifts for them, no welcoming banquets or cries of joy when they were spotted overhead. Rather, there were cries of fear and doors were closed against them.

One day, when Flár spotted Frodleikr flying gracefully up towards the world, his jealousy overcame him and he went to find his sister. "I see that the fount of all knowledge goes once again to bestow his gifts on our father's creations," he sneered.

Hefnd curled her lip. "He does it to spite us," she hissed. "He knows that the creatures do not love us as they do him and he is laughing at us. We should teach him a lesson."

"What do you have in mind?" asked Flár, knowing that Hefnd always had a plan or two in reserve.

"Go and fetch Ofríki and Meinsamr. They can help us," said Hefnd.

Begrudgingly, Flár went off to find the others and they huddled around Hefnd's nest, each voicing their disdain at Frodleikr's behaviour. Ofríki and Meinsamr did not have the same interest in the world as their siblings, so they were less incensed, although they each had their own perceived grievances against their golden brother.

Eventually, it was agreed that they would fly up to the world and steal Frodleikr's stone tablets from one of the races. They set off together in a flash of colour, wings beating against the warm air as they gained height and then soared towards the world, landing at the edge of a beautiful forest. Hefnd knew that Frodleikr often came here, for he was particularly fond of the two races who inhabited the forest. They were innovative and hard-working and he tended to share new discoveries with them first, before visiting other creatures elsewhere on the world. These races were like night and day, for one had skin as pale as Máni's heart and the other had skin as black as Bál's obsidian scales. The pale ones had green eyes, while the dark ones had pure white.

The four siblings set off in search of dwelling places and soon came across a collection of well-made huts near a fast-flowing river. This was the home of the pale creatures, who were busily tending crops, fishing, weaving and building boats. Meinsamr flew over the settlement to distract the creatures while Flár, as the smallest, sneaked to the temple and stole the precious stone tablets that lay within. Meinsamr and Hefnd then landed nearby and began to tell the creatures that Frodleikr had turned against them and had decreed that they no longer deserved the knowledge he had shared with them so generously.

The pale creatures were stunned and confused. "We do not understand," they said, "for Frodleikr gave us new stone tablets this very morning and said nothing to make us suspect that his feelings toward us had changed."

The two dragons sighed heavily, explaining that this was further evidence of Frodleikr's deception. They told the creatures that they had seen Frodleikr removing the tablets from the temple and, at this, several of them ran to the temple to see for themselves, reporting back in devasted voices that the dragons spoke true and the tablets, with all their sacred knowledge, were gone. As the creatures spoke, some of the others began to weep openly, while some became angry and started shouting. Several, however, looked deeply suspicious and said nothing, simply watching as events unfolded.

"Where is this cruel, traitorous Frodleikr?" demanded one of the pale creatures, raising his sword high above his head.

Some of the others clamoured that the golden one had retreated to his favourite clearing, where he was accustomed to rest awhile before journeying on throughout the world. At this, a number of the creatures hurried to arm themselves and, with much shouting, headed off into the forest towards the clearing, with Meinsamr and Hefnd following behind, trying not to let the amusement show on their faces.

Meanwhile, Ofríki and Flár had found a settlement of the dark creatures. Ofríki had caused the distraction and Flár had stolen the stone tablets that lay in their temple. Like their pale cousins, the dark creatures were hurt, angry and confused, but they were more hot-headed and warlike.

Having confirmed that their tablets were, indeed, missing, they immediately armed themselves and set out, knowing Frodleikr would be resting in his clearing before he bade them farewell and left for other parts of the world.

Unseen by either race, Flár flew to the clearing and carefully deposited the tablets next to his sleeping brother before re-joining Ofríki and the dark creatures, who had not noted his absence.

The two races met at opposite ends of the clearing, which was brightly lit by Bál's distant flames as they reflected off his son's golden scales. They saw the tablets lying beside the dragon and their injured cries intensified. Frodleikr awakened as the angry mob approached and watched them as they encircled him with their weapons drawn.

"My friends," he said gently, "why do you come to me thus?"

The leader of the dark creatures stepped forward. "What have we done to make you hate us?" he demanded. "We have ever been your friends, giving you the best of all we had to offer! And now you deem us unworthy and take our sacred tablets without a word of explanation!"

Frodleikr raised himself slightly, causing the assembled creatures to ready themselves against him, but he made no other movement, just regarded them in puzzlement. "My friends," he said again in that same, gentle voice, "why do you think such things of me when you know that I have always been your dearest friend and protector?"

The dark creature pointed at the tablets lying in the grass next to Frodleikr. The dragon frowned and looked where he was pointing. He was deeply shocked when he saw the tablets, for he knew not how they came to be there, and told the creatures so.

The dark ones, however, began to press forward, not allowing him to speak. They leaped onto him and began attacking. Some of the pale ones joined them, striking at the golden scales, which fell like raindrops into the grass below.

Some of the pale creatures hung back, knowing something was not right. Then one of them spotted the other dragons, who were watching from between the trees, smirking. Flár was openly laughing and pointing. The leader of the pale creatures, who was thoughtful and just, realised what had happened and started shouting at the others to stop attacking. He ran forward and started pulling his fellows away from the dragon, shouting at them that it was a trick. Some started helping him, but by this time, they were too late. They managed to stop all their fellows and some of their dark cousins, but the rest were blinded by anger, hurt and betrayal, simply pushing them away and continuing to strike.

During all this, Frodleikr did not retaliate. Large, delicate, gold-flecked tears slid down his face as his friends sliced and pierced and his blood, which glowed with a divine light, began to seep into the ground beneath him.

Suddenly, there was a crash as loud as thunder as Jafnadr and Hreysti landed nearby, their faces contorted with anger and disbelief. The creatures paused, frightened, having never been in the presence of all seven dragons before. They began to exchange worried glances as Jafnadr rounded on his siblings, who had started to back away. "What have you done?" he demanded, his voice heavy with emotion. "What have you done?"

"Nothing," snapped Meinsamr defensively, but Flár, who had always feared his brother's punishments, protested, "It was only in jest!"

Hearing this, the creatures stared at each other in dismay, knowing that they had been tricked in the worst possible way.

"In jest?" repeated Jafnadr incredulously. "We saw you taking the tablets as we flew overhead – you were too preoccupied with your deception to notice us. I knew that you were all capable of great wrongs, but I never imagined anything like this!"

The four huddled together under the onslaught of their brother's righteous fury. "What will you do?" Meinsamr asked fearfully.

"I?" replied Jafnadr. "I will do nothing. You have committed the worst kind of atrocity and have therefore placed yourselves in the hands of a higher authority than I."

The four gasped as the implication of his words hit them and, at that moment, the world suddenly darkened. Everyone stared up at the sky as day turned to night and Bál's flames were hidden from view by the most enormous dragon the creatures had ever seen. So vast that he filled the entire sky, Bál himself hovered above them, his heat searing those below even as his hot tears fell onto the body of his golden son, who lay dying, with his argentate sister at his side.

"You are no children of mine," said Bál in a voice strained with emotion. "I disown and banish you. You are nothing to me. Go. Find the deepest, darkest cavern, the hottest, driest desert or the coldest ocean and hide yourselves in isolation for the rest of your pitiful existence. You are the most despicable creatures I have ever had the misfortune to lay eyes upon. Henceforth, you will be known as the Amáttr, the loathsome, the worst of the worst. Go."

Ofríki started to speak, but Bál silenced him with a roar that caused the earth to tremble and trees to fall. Most of the tiny creatures had fallen to the ground at Bál's appearance and lay there unmoving, sobbing, as Bál screamed his anguish and pain, which was heard throughout the world and caused other races to stop in horror, wondering what such a terrible noise could be.

"You are not worthy to be called my children!" Bál roared. "Get out of my sight and never again show yourselves in my presence. You are banished for all eternity."

There was a long silence. The four, seeing that protest was useless, rose into the air and flew off in different directions.

Bál reached down and gently touched Frodleikr with his long claw. "My son," he wept. "My son, the Virduligr, the magnificent."

Frodleikr raised his eyes, for his body had failed him. "My beloved father," he panted, "do not punish your creatures. They did not know that it was a trick."

The leader of the dark creatures managed to pull himself to his feet and stagger forward, his ears still ringing painfully from Bál's mighty roar. "Our dear friend, what have we done?" he moaned in horror. "Please, please forgive us! What can we do to save you?"

Frodleikr looked at him sadly. "There is nothing that can be done," he said quietly. "It is my time. But I will give you a gift in death, even as I always did in life."

As he spoke, his eyes rolled back and his last breath escaped him.

The silence in the clearing was so profound that it was physically painful to the tiny creatures. Then Jafnadr and Hreysti went to Frodleikr, rested their heads on him and wept. They began a high, keening wail that ululated in the wind and carried to the far corners of the world. Those who heard it knew that something terrible and momentous had come to pass and wondered at it.

Bál's anguish was almost unbearable. To have lost not only his beloved Máni but also his golden son was too much for his heart to bear. Yet he was determined to respect his son's wishes.

"You were misled by those foul things," he said to his tiny creatures. "I will respect his wishes by not wiping you from the face of this world I created. Yet there must be consequences."

He turned to the leader of the pale creatures. "You saw through the deception and stopped many of your cousins from inflicting more damage," he said. "Therefore, your people will remain here in the forest forever, tending to the great temple you will create here in my son's name. You will never live in any other part of this world and those who travel will always be regarded with suspicion. However, I grant you my permission to use the gift my son has left for you. His body may have failed him, but his benevolence towards you was ever unfailing."

At these words, the pale creatures threw themselves to the ground, worshipping the great Bál for his wondrous mercy and dedicating their lives to the worship of his son.

Bál then turned to the leader of the dark creatures.

"You, too, were misled," he said, "yet you did not stop to consider the likely truth of the matter. You refused to listen when others tried to persuade you to stop. From this day forth, you are the worst of the worst. My other creatures will ever shun you and shrink from doing business with you. Anywhere you go, even here in this forest, you will be regarded with hatred and suspicion. As for the gift my son has left, your kind may, perhaps, learn one day to use it, but it will be a struggle. After one hundred generations, that struggle will intensify until one day, your kind will realise that it is gone forever and that you will never get it back. Only then will the terrible loss that has occurred here be truly understood."

So saying, Bál launched himself up into the sky, his huge wings obliterating the light. Eventually, Jafnadr and Hreysti arose and, with a last, sad look at the creatures around them, they unfurled their shining wings and followed their father.

It was dark for seven days and seven nights and all the creatures mourned for the entire time, neither eating nor sleeping, so great was their devastation. The precious stone tablets were returned to their rightful places and the priests began to pray to Frodleikr as they had been instructed by the Great Bál.

From that time on, the dark creatures and their pale cousins have ever been at war and, to this day, neither race ventures far from the security of the forest.

As Frodleikr's body began to return to the earth, joining once more with that of his mother Máni, the pale creatures noticed that a beautiful crop of unusual purple flowers had sprung up in the clearing where he lay. They dug them up to plant around the temple when it was built, but as they removed the plants, they noticed that the earth below was glowing purple. They dug deeper and found the gift Frodleikr had given them – a glowing mineral they had never seen before - although it took many, many years to fully understand its properties and to realise its true potential.

And although the creatures of the forest did not realise, the purple flowers started appearing throughout the world, alerting other races to the Gift, which became known as frodleikite in honour of he who had bestowed it and the great sacrifice he had made.

For Frodleikr's Gift gave them the ability to possess all the knowledge of the world.

The Musician and the Candle-Maker,

or How the Elves got Their Pointed Ears

A long time ago, in the Great Forest of the North, there lived a skilled candle-maker named Zentha. Her people were the Guardians of Dragonheart, the most sacred of all the temples in the Hheserakhian Empire, and Zentha kept the Temple well-supplied with the best of her creations. She was greatly respected for her talents and her kindness, so when she decided to seek a husband, she found there were many men who were keen to join with her.

Zentha was a sensible woman. Rather than rush into anything, she took her time, patiently listening to her suitors and, afterwards, giving careful thought to what they had said. As the weeks went by and she still had not reached a decision, she realised that there was not a single one among them who ignited any sort of spark in her. They were pleasant and good company, she acknowledged, but she could not imagine herself spending the rest of her life with any of them.

The weeks stretched into months and the months stretched into a year and still Zentha had not chosen a suitor. Some of the men had become impatient and started urging her to choose between them, but she resisted, putting them off without really knowing why. There were four or five who would have made her happy, she knew – they were responsible, talented, kind and companionable – but every time she thought about them, she knew something was missing. Plus, they were all so similar that it would have been very difficult to choose one over another when there was really nothing to distinguish any of them.

One day, Zentha was in her workshop as usual, stirring her vat of hot wax, humming gently to herself and thinking about the designs for the batch of candles she was planning for the Temple. The workshop was attached to her house, with a door at the back which led into her living area and one at the front, which her customers used. The whole place smelled pleasantly of candles and there were shelves all along one wall which held examples of Zentha's fine craftsmanship. There were windows in three of the four walls, so it was a beautiful, airy, peaceful place to work. She had placed a trio of chairs near the front door, so that customers had somewhere to sit to discuss their needs and so that she could enjoy a cup of nettle tea with her friends when they passed by and stopped to chat. Every now and then, Zentha would look around her and give thanks to the Great Bál and the Benevolent Frodleikr that she was successful in her work and had the means to live so comfortably.

All of a sudden, she heard a high, sweet melody from somewhere in the forest behind her workshop. She paused in her work, fascinated, for she could not identify the instrument and had never heard the tune before. It was light, airy and magical, twisting and turning like a woodland breeze and it captivated her. She carefully moved the vat from the fire, leaving it close by so the wax wouldn't solidify, then went outside, removing her apron. She unfastened the scarf she wore around her head to keep her long red hair from accidentally falling into the wax as she worked. Hanging the apron on a tree stump by the door, she walked around the side of the building, head tilted to one side as she listened to the music, trying to work out where it was coming from.

Not far from the house, there was a small stream which, at one point, dropped over a ledge about as tall as Zentha and landed in a bubbling pool below before continuing on its way through the forest towards the coast a few miles distant. Zentha and her closest neighbours collected their water from this pool and washed their clothes downstream of it, and Zentha often sat next to the pool in the evenings, sipping nettle tea and enjoying the tranquillity of the forest around her.

Her feet took her down the familiar path and, as she approached the pool, she could tell that the mysterious musician was somewhere nearby. As she drew nearer, she could feel the music inside her, swelling in her chest, caressing her head and tickling a spring into her step. By the time she made her way past the giant flowering shrub which hid the pool from the path, she was almost dancing.

Sitting atop the ledge next to the water, one leg dangling over the edge, was a young man of about her age. Like many of her people, he was tall and slim, with long dark hair and large green eyes which twinkled at her above the unusual instrument he was playing. She stared, trying to work out what it was, for it looked like a straight, pale stick.

Seeing her curiosity, he winked at her and ended the melody with a flourish before rising to his feet and bowing to her. He moved with a fluid grace and she found herself blushing and peeping up at him from beneath her eyelashes as she dropped into a curtsey.

"Good day to you, fair maid," he called. His voice was deep and melodious and sent a thrill through her. "I am Jonik, of the Clan of Three Oaks."

"Good day to you, sir. I am Zentha of Dragonheart," she replied.

Jonik smiled. "I am delighted to make your acquaintance," he said. "I have reached Dragonheart, then. I wondered if I was nearby."

"You are on a pilgrimage?" asked Zentha. Dragonheart was well-used to those from other Clans making the trek south to worship or seek healing or knowledge from the priests. She made special votive candles to sell to pilgrims, after being approached several years previously by a particularly pious woman from the distant northern coast, who had discovered that the candles she had brought with her had been damaged on the journey. Zentha had just finished preparing a batch of tiny candles which she was intending to use to test new dyes. The woman spotted them and immediately bought the entire batch. After that, people started coming to her regularly asking for prayer candles, so she had gladly added them to her wares.

"In a manner of speaking," Jonik said. "I travel often, for my music prefers to be on the move, rather than confined at home. Three Oaks is beautiful, but the forest has so many wonders."

"It does," agreed Zentha enthusiastically. "Its personality changes wherever you go, as does its face. Here in Dragonheart, we have clearings full of flowers, beautiful streams and gentle slopes for our crops. But further east, there are mountains, deep ravines and, I have heard, very few streams."

"And in the north," said Jonik, "there are long expanses of flat land all along the coast, where our cousins set up their fishing lines. Miles and miles of land so flat, you'd swear it was a table-top!"

Zentha laughed. "I think I would like to see the fisher-folk of the north," she said. "But please tell me...what is that instrument you play? I have never seen its like before, nor heard such sweet music."

Jonik stooped to pick up a bag next to his feet and jumped down from the top of the waterfall, landing softly in front of her. He held out the instrument and she saw immediately that it was, indeed, a stick, which had been carefully smoothed. "What kind of stick is that?" she exclaimed.

"This is a reed pipe," he told her. "Here, try it." He moved around behind her and guided her hands so that she found herself fitting her fingers over the holes and blowing into the pipe to make the notes. It was difficult at first, for it was entirely unfamiliar to her, but at one point, she managed to make a single, pure note. Laughing delightedly, she turned to face him and found that he was still standing close behind her, his smile mirroring her own as he enjoyed the pleasure she found in her little triumph. They stared into each other's eyes for a long moment before Zentha self-consciously stepped back slightly. "Thank you for showing me," she said.

"If you would like to learn, I will be happy to teach you," he said with another of his dazzling smiles.

Zentha invited him to accompany her to her workshop for some refreshment, which he gladly accepted. They walked together along the path, conversing easily about his journey, the community of Dragonheart, music and candles. He was fascinated to hear what she did and when they arrived at the workshop, he wandered up and down the room, looking at each of the different candles, asking questions about the designs and the process of creation. Even when she had made tea, he did not sit down, but continued admiring her work as he sipped the refreshing brew.

Zentha, seeing his fascination, repositioned her vat of wax and built up the fire, finding that it was easy to answer his questions as she worked. She showed him how to stir the wax and when it was exactly the right consistency, then let him add the dye. It was only when she glanced up to see the light outside was fading that she realised they had spent the entire afternoon together. It had seemed like no time at all.

Jonik found himself somewhere to stay and started courting Zentha. They found that they were well-matched in almost every respect and, before long, Zentha knew she had found her soulmate. They were married one bright spring day and the Clan held a huge banquet to celebrate their union.

Life soon settled into a comfortable routine. Zentha worked on new designs and Jonik helped by mixing the dyes. He composed beautiful melodies for her, which he played while she worked. At first, Zentha found the music distracting, for she was so entranced that she kept stopping to listen and forgot what she was supposed to be doing. Over time, however, she grew used to her beloved sitting on the corner of the table, his fingers dancing across the reed pipe, and eventually, found that she became more distracted when he wasn't there, playing for her. Some of the Clan leaders, having heard him play, engaged him as a tutor to their children. As well as teaching Zentha, he also had a healthy number of young pupils and the Clan greatly enjoyed listening to the enchanting music weaving its way through the trees as they went about their daily chores. It lifted their spirits and brought smiles to their faces. The Clan leaders found that they were dealing with far fewer disputes and crimes since Jonik had joined their number and they were all grateful to him for the wonderful benefit his music brought to them.

One day, Jonik was playing his pipe for Zentha while she bathed in the stream. It was a beautiful, sunny day and the pair were celebrating, for Zentha was with child. As he played, Jonik thought how beautiful and talented his wife was and how very fortunate he was to have met her.

That afternoon, however, Zentha was not the only one enchanted by Jonik's music. A skogsra, one of the spirits who dwelled within the forest, happened to be nearby and heard the sweet melody as it carried on the breeze. Curious, she drew nearer to see what it was.

When she saw Jonik, and heard him play, she immediately wanted him for herself. She flitted between the leaves and from shadow to dappled shadow, until she was close enough to reach out and gently touch the ends of his long dark hair, marvelling at how soft it was. She tilted her head in time to the melody, letting out a little cry when it ended abruptly as Jonik rose to his feet. Peering through the leaves, the skogsra saw why he had stopped. There was a woman. Judging by the way he was looking at her, he loved her very much. The skogsra allowed herself a tight, hard smile. He wouldn't feel that way much longer.

Zentha had heard the skogsra's cry when Jonik stopped playing. As he jumped down with her towel and helped her step carefully out of the stream, she asked, "Did you hear something when you stopped playing?"

"Only the sound of you splashing," he teased as he wrapped her in a towel. "Come, my love. Let us return home. I have a pupil later, but until then, I will read to you while you work."

The two moved away, leaving the skogsra plotting.

As the time drew near for Zentha's baby to be born, she became increasingly worried that something was wrong. Over the last few weeks, she had noticed that her tools seemed to be moving by themselves. She would leave them on the table or her workbench, only to find them gone when she returned. Sometimes, she would find them in strange places — sticking up in her vegetable garden, in a drawer, under her pillow. Not only that, but jars were mysteriously knocked over, bowls of dye were spoiled and an entire batch of candles had to be melted down as the wax had somehow become dirty, as though they had been kicked around a dusty path. Yet Zentha had only been out of the room for a matter of minutes while she made herself some tea.

Concerned, she told Jonik. He had been spending less time in her workshop as other Clans were now sending him pupils and he had a thriving teaching practice, of which Zentha was very proud. He immediately offered to join her while she worked, so they could keep watch together and see if they could find out why these strange things were happening.

However, to Zentha's frustration, nothing whatsoever occurred while Jonik was with her, yet when he wasn't there, Zentha would find her knife had vanished, or her tea had been spilled. Once, an apron nearly caught fire because it had been moved closer to the hearth. Jonik urged her to stop working so hard and this upset Zentha, because it was clear that he thought she was imagining things. She was becoming more tired, for it was almost her time, but she liked to be active, so she cut down a little on new creations and busied herself with stocking up on old favourites and prayer candles. However, the strange events continued, so Zentha knew something was afoot.

When the baby arrived, Zentha and Jonik's joy knew no limits. They adored their tiny daughter and, after much consideration, named her Ljómi, which means radiance. Jonik spent hours cradling her on her lap, playing soothing, gentle melodies to help her sleep. Zentha, watching from her chair, had never felt happier or more content in her life and knew that she was truly blessed.

One day, Zentha was finishing preparations for their evening meal. Jonik had had a full day of teaching and was due home very shortly. Baby Ljómi was sleeping peacefully on a bed of the softest rabbit skins, gurgling to herself every now and then. Zentha hummed as she sliced bread and set out some beautiful berries she had found earlier when she took Ljómi for a walk in the forest.

As the sky darkened and Jonik had not appeared, Zentha became concerned. She carefully strapped the sleeping baby to her back and went to the houses of the Clan members whose children were her husband's pupils. She discovered that he had seen all of them and had left the last one to return home. Worried now, she hurried home, but the house was dark and empty. She ran to the stream to see if he was there, but there was no sign of him. Fighting back tears, she turned towards home, but as she did so, her foot struck something in the grass. She stooped to pick it up and felt the blood run cold in her veins. It was Jonik's precious reed pipe, lying abandoned in the grass.

For a long while, Zentha stood frozen, staring numbly at the instrument she held. The baby stirred and awakened, jerking her back to herself. She returned to the house, fed the baby and managed to choke down some bread, then set out once more into the forest with a lantern and Jonik's pipe. Every so often, she would stop, set the lantern down and play, in the hope that her husband would hear her. She feared that he was injured, or perhaps lost. Something must have startled him if he had dropped his reed pipe. She clung to the hope that he would hear the music and signal to her somehow.

Zentha found nothing that night, nor the next day, nor the night that followed. Day and night, she ventured out, searching, searching for her lost love. Her friends grew concerned when they saw her, for she looked thin and tired and her beloved candles lay scattered untidily about her workshop, abandoned and forgotten. Since Jonik's disappearance, nothing unusual had happened in the workshop and Zentha was more convinced than ever that some malicious entity had sought to do her harm. She racked her brains to try to work out what she might have done to anger a spirit, but could think of nothing.

One night, many weeks after Jonik had vanished, Zentha was tending to baby Ljómi, who had woken up and was crying. As she paced, rocking her daughter gently to sleep, Zentha happened to glance out of the window. What she saw made her stop and stare.

A strange creature was moving about in her garden. From the front, it seemed to be a beautiful woman, but when it turned, Zentha saw that it had a tail rather like a cow's and its back resembled tree bark. It was pulling some of the vegetables from her garden and flinging them away, then stamping on others.

Zentha watched in horror as the creature worked its malice and then vanished into the forest as silently as it had arrived.

The next day, Zentha was working in the garden, trying to repair the damage, when one of her friends, Aravae, arrived. Puzzled, she stared at the devastation.

"What on earth has happened?" she exclaimed, hurrying over to help as best she could. Together the friends worked as Zentha told her everything that had happened. As she spoke, Aravae's eyes widened.

"Oh, my dear," she said in a hushed voice, "that must have been the skogsra, Háski! I have heard tales of her, but am glad to say that I have never seen her."

"Háski?" gasped Zentha. "I know of her, of course...but I thought the Hidden Folk were simply a legend."

"Oh no, it's not a legend, unfortunately," replied Aravae grimly. "Let us go inside. I will show you how to banish her."

Zentha was distraught, for she knew that Háski and her kind preyed on unsuspecting men in the forest, placing them under a spell and seducing them. The thought that her dearest Jonik was in that foul creature's clutches was almost more than she could bear, but Zentha was a strong woman and it wasn't long before anger and practicality took over. She followed Aravae's instructions, donning gloves to make posies of poisonous tibast and valerian leaves and pinning one to her apron, then she pounded some of their roots in a mortar to make a potion, which she carefully sealed in a bottle and placed on a shelf.

That night, Zentha was prepared. She pretended that she had gone to bed, but once the lights were out, she sat near the window, taking care that she could not be seen, and watched for the skogsra. Háski did not come that night, nor the next, but on the third, she appeared just after midnight and spent a few minutes digging out the vegetables again. Zentha watched with gritted teeth as all her hard work was ruined, but she bided her time, waiting for the creature to tire of the sport and return to her lair.

As soon as Háski set off, Zentha lost no time in following her. The skogsra wound her way through the trees in such a haphazard way that Zentha feared she might be unable to find her way back. The moon was bright that night, for which she was glad.

All at once, Zentha spotted a clearing ahead and her heart started pounding in her chest. The creature approached a large hollow oak tree, from which a familiar figure suddenly emerged. Jonik! Zentha almost cried out, but her voice caught in her throat as she saw her beloved embrace the creature, seemingly oblivious to anything around him. Watching how he moved, Zentha understood that he was under the foul skogsra's spell, for he looked like he was sleepwalking. His usual elegance and grace was gone, replaced by a bumbling shuffle that broke Zentha's heart and made her even more determined to break the skogsra's hold over him and bring him back to the safety of their home.

The baby stirred and, anxious that she should not be discovered, Zentha crept away, leaving her husband in the skogsra's embrace. She fought back tears as she returned to her house, using her knife to make discreet marks on the tree trunks to guide her back to the creature's lair.

The following day, Zentha left the baby in Aravae's care. Returning home, she packed up some bread, cheese and ale in a bag, donned her gloves and ensured that the posy of tibast and valerian was securely attached to her apron. She carefully placed the second posy in the bag and, taking Jonik's reed pipe, she set out determinedly towards the skogsra's lair. Following the marks on the tree trunks, she made her way quickly and easily to the lair and found a hiding place between a dense shrub and the trunk of a gnarled old oak. She waited and watched for some time, but there was no sign of life. Tentatively, making sure that she was well hidden and that she had a clear path behind her should she need to flee, Zentha removed her gloves, raised the reed pipe to her lips and began to play.

For the longest time, nothing happened. Zentha played on, tear-filled eyes fixed on the hollow tree. She was relieved that at least the skogsra had not appeared and dared to hope that her plan might actually succeed. Cautiously, the pipe still to her lips, she rose and slowly approached the hollow tree.

As she neared, she heard movement and the melody faltered for a moment as she started and caught her breath. However, she recognised the shuffling steps from within the tree and, taking a deep breath, she continued to play as her husband wandered out of the gloom, blinking in the sunlight. He was dirty and dishevelled, his clothes unwashed and stained. His gaze wandered around the clearing, passing over Zentha but not settling, as though she were not even there.

Zentha slowly approached him as she finished the final bars of the melody. She slipped the pipe into her pocket and, wrapping her hand in her apron for speed, took the second posy from her bag, then reached out and carefully, pinned it to Jonik's shirt. He watched in bemused acceptance and when she took his hand and started gently leading him away, he followed her docilely. As they walked together, Zentha watched closely for any sign that the spell was loosening its grip on him, but as they reached home and he remained unchanged, she realised that he was so deeply bewitched that she might have lost him forever. She helped him to change his clothes and wash, then settled him in bed and went downstairs. Aravae arrived a while later with baby Ljómi and, on hearing what had happened, warned Zentha to be on her guard. The skogsra would be angered to find that her plaything had gone and would undoubtedly seek revenge. Zentha nodded grimly. She had expected no less and would be ready.

That night, Zentha was downstairs with the baby, who was sleeping peacefully on her little bed of rabbit skins. She had tried to keep herself busy with some mending, but it lay forgotten at her feet, so great was her distraction. Every noise made her start and eventually, she took to pacing quietly, glancing across to the table where the potion bottle was standing ready.

Finally, after an agony of waiting, Zentha heard footsteps approaching swiftly and, a moment later, her door was flung wide. The skogsra stood in the doorway, her beautiful face contorted with rage and jealousy. "Where is he?" she cried in a voice as harsh as rocks. "What have you done with my love?"

"I have brought him back to the home you stole him from," Zentha answered firmly.

The skogsra let out a shrill cry of rage and leaped at Zentha, who screamed and flung herself backwards towards the window, away from the door. Baby Ljómi awoke and started crying and Zentha's blood suddenly ran cold as she realised that the creature was now standing between the baby and the table and she herself was no longer within reach of either. She could lunge forward and either grab the potion from the table, or the baby from its furs. She could not do both.

As she stood, poised to flee or fight, the creature made the decision for her. She rushed at Zentha, who had no choice but to dodge to her right. However, as it reached her, the creature let out a wail when it saw the posy on Zentha's apron and recoiled back a step or two, which allowed Zentha to reach Ljómi and scoop her up. Outside, she could hear running footsteps and shouting as her neighbours, alerted by the noise, began to investigate. She was about to shout out to them when Háski, quick as lightning, grabbed the baby and tried to pull her out of Zentha's arms. Zentha screamed in fury, holding on to Ljómi as tightly as she could while the creature did its best to drag the child away.

The footsteps outside grew louder as Zentha struggled and Aravae suddenly appeared, her father behind her. She stopped in the doorway, horrified at the sight before her.

"Get the bottle!" screamed Zentha desperately, feeling her grip on her daughter weakening. The skogsra laughed maliciously and hissed at Aravae, who let out a shrill shriek and cringed away. Zentha tried to elbow the creature aside so she could move closer to the table, but Háski, realising what she was trying to do, redoubled her efforts to steal the baby, laughing gleefully the whole time. "I shall have them both!" she cackled delightedly. "Your husband is now mine and I shall have your child too!"

"Never!" came a voice from behind Zentha.

A moment later, Háski let out a scream of pain and fury as the potion was splashed over her. Her grip loosened slightly, but she grabbed the child's ears, making Ljómi scream even more loudly.

"I curse you all!" shrieked Háski. "I curse you all! From this day forward, you and all your kind will suffer your baby's affliction!" With that, she turned and fled, shoving Aravae and her father out of her way and pushing through the crowd of neighbours who had gathered outside. All of them saw her back and tail as she hurried away and there were cries of fear and disgust. More than one person reached for a protective amulet as they realised what they had encountered.

Zentha sank to the floor, holding Ljómi tight to her breast, blinded by tears, wondering what the skogsra had meant by "affliction", for her child was perfectly healthy. All at once, the events of the last few moments hit her and she raised her head to see her beloved Jonik standing by the table, the empty potion bottle still in his hand and his eyes fixed on the doorway. He turned to look at her and she saw immediately that the spell was broken.

"Jonik! My love!" she sobbed.

He knelt and took her in his arms, his tears mingling with her own as he cradled her and their child, rocking them gently. "You saved me," he repeated over and over. "I could hear your screams, I heard Ljómi crying….it was as though I was in a terrible nightmare. I knew I had to help you, yet nothing felt real. It was only when I saw her…her back…and her tail," he faltered, then wept again.

Aravae's father crossed the room and, leaning down, tilted Jonik's face up towards his own and peered closely at him. He snapped his fingers right in front of Jonik's eyes and when he blinked and recoiled, he stepped back, satisfied. "The spell is broken," he announced confidently. "You saw her back and her tail?" Jonik nodded wordlessly. "Then you are now immune to her advances, should you be unfortunate enough to cross her path again."

Their neighbours, recovering from the fright, bustled their way in and took over, wrapping the couple in blankets, building up the fire, settling them in chairs and making tea. Aravae carefully wrapped baby Ljómi in her furs and brought her to her mother, who clasped her beloved daughter and rocked her gently until she finally fell asleep. By that time, their neighbours, satisfied that the family were now safe, had returned home. Zentha carried the sleeping child upstairs and the three of them curled up together and fell asleep.

In the morning, Zentha awoke first and looked down at Ljómi, who was sleeping in the crook of her arm. Something was wrong and it took a moment for her sleepy mind to understand what she was seeing. When she realised, she screamed in horror.

For where the skogsra's long, thin fingers had touched the baby's ears, they had been pulled out of shape and were now long and pointed. Zentha leaped out of bed, awakening Jonik and Ljómi. Horrified, she saw that Jonik also had long pointed ears and when she raised her hands to her head, she felt the new shape of her own ears.

As they stared at each other numbly, they could hear distant screams and shouts from others in the community as they, too, awakened to the effects of Háski's curse.

 The Clan never saw Háski again and it took them a long time to come to terms with the effects of her curse. The leaders consulted great wizards in an attempt to reverse it, but to no avail. The curse was irreversible. They were destined to live forever more with long, pointed ears and, as they later learned, so were their great enemies, their dark cousins from the east of the forest, for Háski's curse had included all their kind.

Once it became apparent that they could do nothing to change the curse, the Clan had no choice but to begrudgingly accept their fate. Eventually, however, they grew to love their new ears. Their hearing became far more acute, bringing their hunters greater success and enabling them to feed the Clan well. Their guards were more effective as they could now hear a threat long before it reached them. The Clan as a whole began to develop a deep affinity with the natural world around them, for they could now distinguish between the footfall of a fox and a badger and hear changes within the wind that signalled inclement weather. Their farming improved and they had better goods with which to trade. Merchants found that they were being cheated less often. Politicians could distinguish the words in whispered conversations and, after a few generations had passed, Elven assassins were the most highly desired in the Empire.

Jonik and Zentha lived happily together with their children for the rest of their days. Jonik's music became even more captivating as he could now distinguish even the tiniest difference between notes and hear music in the stream, the wind, the rustling leaves, laughter and the sounds of the birds and animals around him. He became widely celebrated as a great musician and began to give public performances, where he commanded great audiences. Zentha continued to create candles and her increasingly intricate designs became highly sought after in religious centres throughout the Empire. Ljómi, who, fortunately, had suffered no ill effects from that traumatic, life-changing night, grew to be a skilled woodcarver.

Now, the Elves see their ears as a badge of honour, the mark of a people of strength, determination and deep love. There is no evil which cannot be destroyed by a parent's bond with their child.

Death's Fingers

A long time ago, there was a witch named Langlifr who was obsessed with the dark arts. She was not interested in helping people to understand their future, or to bless the soil in a farmer's field to improve the yield of crops. She had no time for glamours, although she did, on occasion, transform herself into a crow when it served her purpose. She had no interest in the pursuit of gold. What she truly wanted was dark indeed – an army of the reanimated dead, before which all kings and emperors would bow down as they relinquished their power to her. Then, as ruler of the entire world, all races would be hers to command and control, to maintain or destroy, to bestow honours or devastate lives.

Langlifr had long had this ambition, which developed into an all-consuming quest. Many years previously, she had acquired an ancient scroll detailing a blood ritual which had been outlawed for centuries. The scroll was badly damaged, but the faded, spidery writing was just about legible. Langlifr spent hours studying it, her nose almost touching the parchment, learning all she could about the ritual and the necromancer who created it. She listed the various ingredients, tools and artefacts she would need to conduct the ritual and systematically started gathering them, travelling all over the world in a variety of disguises and stopping at nothing to get what she wanted.

Eventually, just three items separated her from her vision.

One was Hefnd's Cup, a notorious and mythical vessel which no living creature had ever set eyes upon. It was believed that the wicked dragon Hefnd, sister to the noble Frodleikr, had carved the Cup from the trunk of a tree which was soaked in her brother's blood after his tragic and violent death. Anyone who owned and drank from the Cup would have infinite power bestowed upon them and it was vital to the ritual. When she started investigating, Langlifr was taken aback by the sheer number of legends attached to the Cup. The dragons believed that possessing it would bring nothing but ill-fortune of the very worst kind, while drinking from it meant instant death. A religious order in the southernmost part of the Hheserakhian Empire believed that their temple was the rightful home of the Cup and when it was finally brought back to them, it would herald the return of Frodleikr, with the righteous being granted entry to Paradise and the sinful being brought to account for their wrongdoing. One or two dwarven legends referred to the Cup as the Life-Giver, while others in different parts of the world claimed that it held the "cursed brew" which would inflict an eternal, vampiric half-life on anyone who drank from it.

The second item was even more enigmatic. Referred to as simply "the instrument", it was frustratingly absent from any of the necromancer's other papers and Langlifr had eventually exhausted the few lines of enquiry she had managed to uncover. She had no idea what kind of instrument it was. Ritual? Musical? Scientific? All she could do was hope that one of the other two items would somehow lead her to it.

The last of the missing items should really have been the most straightforward to locate. It was a mineral known as Death's Fingers, a milky-white crystal which formed in the shape of a grotesque skeletal hand. However, it was incredibly rare. While travelling, Langlifr found that the known deposits of Death's Fingers had been entirely depleted and some magical practitioners were calling for the crystal to be re-classified as extinct.

Alarmed at this discovery, Langlifr immediately set about making enquiries. Initially, she turned up several promising leads, some in other countries, but on every occasion, the crystals had either been misidentified or the deposit she had been told about didn't exist. She was not the only person hunting for Death's Fingers and some of the seekers were sabotaging the efforts of anyone they felt might beat them to the prize. Langlifr discovered the identity of one saboteur and invited him to the room she had taken at an inn. The following morning, he was found by the innkeeper, cowering in a corner, gibbering incoherently, his hair turned snow white. Of Langlifr, there was no sign.

For a while, Langlifr could find no new clues about any of the three items and she grew increasingly impatient and ill-tempered as the months passed and she had no fresh information about any of them. That all changed, however, when she returned to her home in the Hheserakhian Empire after being away for many years on her fruitless quest.

She had taken some of her papers to the local inn and was sitting at a table poring over them, a flagon of beer at her elbow. No one paid her much attention, although a couple

44

of wizards, who glanced down at her papers as they passed, suddenly decided that they needed to be elsewhere and left in a hurry without even reaching the bar. The innkeeper frowned after them, but on glancing round the bar and seeing nothing except some regulars and a woman reading some papers, he shrugged and went back to work. A large group of dwarves had just arrived and he quickly sent his assistant to bring up another barrel of strong ale from the cellar.

The dwarves settled around the tables next to Langlifr and immediately started a noisy, lively conversation about the day's work. It seemed that they all worked for a local landowner called Calix Bloodshard, who was cousin to almost all of them and who owned most of the mines in the area. Langlifr, at the mention of mines, focussed in on their conversation in the hope of learning something new, but tuned out again as they argued about the relative quality of different types of granite and had a shouting match about which of them loved sapphires the most. The innkeeper kept them well-supplied with ale and they grew increasingly loud and rowdy as the evening went on. Eventually, Langlifr began to gather her papers and picked up her flagon to drain it, just as one of the dwarves said loudly, "...next to Death's Fingers."

Langlifr's hand shook and some of the beer slopped onto the table, narrowly missing the papers. She carefully set the flagon down again, listening intently. The dwarves were all working in one of Bloodshard's mines and had hit a new seam of gold. As they were working on it, they had uncovered a new tunnel leading to a large cavern, which had almost immediately yielded a beautiful sapphire, so they had spent some time investigating. Nothing else had come to light except a strange, milky-white formation in the centre of the cavern which they fervently believed was Death's Fingers.

As soon as the conversation had swerved onto the subject of gold, Langlifr finished her beer, gathered her papers and left the inn. She headed for the docks, where Ansgar the assayer had his premises. No lights were on, but Langlifr knew that the assayer, like many other tradespeople, lived above his workshop. She knocked on the door until Ansgar appeared, bleary-eyed and irritable from being rudely awakened late at night. When he saw Langlifr, however, he was instantly awake and answered her questions carefully and politely, hugely relieved when his answers seemed to satisfy her. After she left, he put a chair under his door handle before returning to bed...just in case.

Langlifr now knew which mine she was looking for. Ironfist, the most profitable of all the mines in Bloodshard's portfolio.

She knew Bloodshard by reputation. He was one of the wealthiest dwarves alive and in his three hundred years, he had vastly improved the standing of his extensive family, albeit through greed and intimidation. As he approached the end of his life, his many relatives were rubbing their hands in glee at the thought of the riches that would come their way after his passing. Such was his nature that it was unlikely he would be mourned by many.

Langlifr made her way to the Ironfist mine, which was at the foot of the mountains several miles distant. There were a dozen or so dwarves around the entrance, some breaking up rocks, others loading some kind of ore into carts, and a foreman shouting orders. She managed to slip into the mine unnoticed and began making her way down the damp, narrow passages, all the while looking out for any sign of Death's Fingers. She quickly realised how vast the mine was and began leaving little marks in the rock, above the dwarves' eyeline, so she could find her way out again.

The passages wound round and round and down, sometimes opening into huge caverns and sometimes narrowing so much that she could only just squeeze herself through. She walked and walked, hiding every now and then when she heard the sound of approaching footsteps. There was no sign of Death's Fingers anywhere, it was unbearably hot in the mine and her feet were starting to ache. She decided that she would stop and rest in the next cavern she came to.

The next cavern was some distance away, but when she reached it, she could hear, very faintly, the sound of pickaxes busily working away at the rock beyond. She found a small space behind a large boulder where she was unlikely to be spotted and sank down gratefully onto the dusty ground. Retrieving her papers from her bag, she re-read her notes about Death's Fingers in the hope of finding a clue about where she was most likely to locate the crystal. She cast a tiny light on the end of one finger and sat squinting at the pages, a deep frown creasing her brow. Finding nothing of use, she sighed and returned the papers to her bag, extinguishing her light just as a set of loud footsteps rang out along the passage, heading her way. The footsteps passed through the cavern and retreated along another tunnel.

Langlifr waited until it was quiet and then left her hiding place, looking around the cavern thoughtfully. She was definitely in the right place, she realised excitedly, for she could see the glimmer of gold running in a wide band around part of the cavern wall and there were tools lying around. She wondered where the miners were. Perhaps they had gone to explore one of the tunnels. She had entered the cavern from the tunnel to her left and there were three others leading from it. She contemplated each of them for a moment, then shrugged and chose the right-hand tunnel. She paused to make a small mark above the tunnel mouth before heading off to see where it led.

This part of the mine was darker than the rest and there was no sign of the miners, which pleased her. There were lanterns, but these were spaced more widely, providing isolated pools of soft bioluminescence in an otherwise inky darkness. Langlifr was forced to slow her steps, for the ground was uneven. She suspected that this was an exploratory tunnel, for it was clearly not being worked. Her heart beat a little faster as she wondered when she would reach the extent of the dwarves' explorations. Was this the tunnel she had heard about in the inn?

As she made her way along a particularly dark section, Langlifr noticed a soft white glow up ahead. It was very different from the bioluminescent lanterns and she caught her breath, trying not to get too excited. The glow grew a little brighter as she approached and she eventually saw that it was coming from a side tunnel. She paused to leave a mark above the tunnel mouth and then continued on towards the source of the light.

The tunnel sloped downwards slightly and Langlifr was encouraged to see that there were no lanterns hanging from its walls. The light ahead grew a little brighter as she neared and she could see that the tunnel curved around to the right. She rounded the corner and found herself in a long, low cavern with a huge formation of Death's Fingers almost in the centre of it, right in front of her.

Langlifr was frozen to the spot for a moment, her eyes wide and her mouth agape as she drank in the sheer splendour of the crystal. It looked as though a thousand tortured souls had been frozen in time as they clawed at the remnants of their existence, their twisted fingers hooked around nothingness. What a truly incredible sight, she thought. After all these years and all the false leads, all the miles I have travelled...I finally have it. It is mine!

She hurried to the crystal, making her way around it, appraising it from every angle before deciding which part to take. One section resembled three skeletal arms twisted around each other and she examined it closely, finally deciding where she should strike it in order to sever it. She knelt down to get her tools from her bag.

"So the men were right. We do have an intruder. What are you doing?"

Langlifr started as the stentorian voice rang through the cavern. The crystal reverberated, a painful, bassy thrum.

"I said what are you doing?" the voice demanded. Langlifr looked around the crystal and saw a dwarf standing just inside the cavern mouth, a large axe in his hands. She guessed that this was Calix Bloodshard, for he was richly dressed and exuded power.

"What is it to you what I am doing? It does not concern you," she replied, noticing how the crystal sang in a different key in response to her voice – a lighter, more musical note.

Bloodshard uttered a short, barking laugh that the crystal echoed with a violent shudder. "You are trespassing in my mine and appear intent on theft," he retorted. "I think that is most definitely my concern."

The crystal responded in its low voice again, but this time, Langlifr heard an ominous crack and caught her breath. Was the sound of their voices enough to shatter Death's Fingers? She would have to take great care.

She shrugged, playing for time. Her mind was racing. How to get the crystal without revealing anything to the dwarf? She couldn't attack him or do anything which made a loud noise, as that might destroy the crystal and she could not take that risk.

"Why are you interested in that crystal?" Bloodshard persisted. "Answer, or you will feel the bite of my blade!"

Langlifr quickly ran through everything she had heard about Bloodshard and suddenly hit on a plan that would distract him and enable her to get away with the crystal. "Oh, very well," she scowled. "I need some of this crystal for a spell that gives eternal life."

"Eternal life?" Bloodshard repeated, his curiosity evident in his voice. The axe lowered a little as he turned his attention to the crystal. "What spell?"

Langlifr launched into a long and detailed description of her research in various magical archives across the world and her discovery of an ancient scroll by an unknown but extremely learned and skilled sorcerer. Much of what she said was true. She just made up the spell the scroll contained. She wove him a beautiful description of a complex ritual which granted eternal life and in which Death's Fingers played an important role. She deliberately didn't tell him just how vital it was to her plans, for she knew he would then have power over her. No one had power over Langlifr.

Bloodshard cocked his head to one side as he listened, his expression sceptical. "So," he said when she had finished, "what are you, then, some sort of witch?"

Langlifr felt an angry snarl rise in her throat at the insult, but managed to control herself. "I am Langlifr," she said pointedly.

The dwarf raised an eyebrow. "Oh, I think I've heard of you," he said, dismissively. "Something about a dragon and a necromancer. Was that you?"

Langlifr cringed inside at the memory of that awful time in her long life, an incident she had worked hard to obliterate from her memory. His words felt like she had torn open a wound and it was a moment before she could reply. Fighting to control her anger, she said levelly, "Perhaps."

Bloodshard regarded her for a moment. He had lowered his axe and was stroking his long, luxurious white beard, his eyes narrowed in thought. Langlifr watched him calmly, but in her head, she was frantically going through her catalogue of spells, trying to find one that would incapacitate but not make any noise when cast. She couldn't think of a single one. His casual insult had truly roused her ire and she was struggling with her inner turmoil. Langlifr was well known – some might even say notorious – so it was highly unlikely that the dwarf had never heard of her. Her indignation and pride clouded her judgment and she did not immediately register that Bloodshard was toying with her.

Eventually, he said, "So it appears we have a situation here. I have something that you want, but you have something that I am interested in."

"And what might that be?" asked Langlifr shortly.

"I am old," Bloodshard said frankly. "My family are circling like vultures to get their hands on my gold. I have spent my life building my fortune, while they have done nothing except wait."

Langlifr shrugged. "Then spend it," she suggested.

Bloodshard chuckled. "You clearly have no idea of how wealthy I am or how long it would take to spend that amount of money."

"Donate it to your temple," Langlifr shot back.

"My money paid for my temple," Bloodshard said, "and the High Priest receives a generous amount each month to ensure that it is well-maintained."

"Give it to the poor," Langlifr said indifferently, turning her attention back to the crystal. She really wasn't interested in some narcissistic dwarf with too much gold. She would get the crystal, by force if she had to. She wondered if wrapping it in something would dull the effect of the sound waves.

"That is the very thing I am keen to avoid," Bloodshard retorted. "My entire family present themselves as 'the poor' and expect me to buy them this or that. I am besieged with petitions every single day. Dozens of them. And that is just from my family. Even my most demanding tenants are less needy."

"Sounds like you have a large family," remarked Langlifr nonchalantly. Bloodshard sighed heavily.

"Two hundred and eighty-seven living relatives," he said sourly. "Another one was born last week. Two hundred and eighty-seven lazy, grasping relatives who are content to watch me work myself to death while they lounge around doing nothing but waiting for me to die."

Langlifr sighed and shook her head in a semblance of solidarity, hoping it would encourage Bloodshard to keep talking. It did. He launched into a long description of some of the ridiculous things his family had expected him to fund and, as he talked, Langlifr's plan became fully formed. She knew what he wanted from her and she would gladly give it in return for the crystal – but the last laugh would be hers.

Eventually Bloodshard got to the point. "If I could only outlive them all," he said. "That really would be the ultimate revenge. I would pay good money just to see the expression on their faces when they realised that there would be no inheritance."

"All I ask in return is as much of the Death's Fingers crystal as I need for my task," Langlifr replied.

Bloodshard blinked and stared at her. "You'll do it?" he asked in disbelief. Langlifr forced herself to smile disarmingly.

"Of course," she said. "After all, like you said, each of us has something the other wants."

Bloodshard gave a delighted laugh. "Let's get started, then!" he exclaimed. "What do you need to do?"

Langlifr had to fight against a powerful urge to roll her eyes. She quickly rattled off a list of instructions, after which Bloodshard handed her the large ruby ring he wore and then helped her to shear off the desired section of Death's Fingers. It was heavier than either of them expected and Langlifr was obliged to cast a spell so that the crystal floated alongside her as she followed Bloodshard out of the cavern and back up to the surface so that she could work the spell for him.

At the surface, Langlifr led Bloodshard to her workshop and began preparing the spell. Bloodshard watched, fascinated, as the ritual progressed. When Langlifr held out the ruby ring for him to put on, he hesitated a little.

"What's the matter?" asked Langlifr. "Don't you want to see those two hundred and eighty-seven faces when they realise they won't get your money?"

Bloodshard pressed his lips together in determination, took the ring and placed it firmly on his finger. "Thank you," he said.

"Just remember," Langlifr said as he made his way to the door, "you must never take that ring off or the spell will be broken and you will die. Never let anyone know the secret of your long life, for there are many unscrupulous people who would think nothing of taking your finger along with the ring!"

Bloodshard assured her that he would not tell a soul, then he thanked her once again and left. After he had gone, Langlifr sat at her table and laughed until tears rolled down her cheeks. Bloodshard was so intent on revenging his grasping family that he hadn't even noticed that she hadn't used the Death's Fingers in the ritual. Still, she thought, as she reached for her papers and carefully unwrapped the crystal, he would get what he wanted. He would outlive his two hundred and eighty-seven relatives, just not in the way he expected. And once he realised the truth, he would be powerless to do anything about it.

The first death came just three days later. Bloodshard was shocked when one of his cousins, a couple of hundred years his junior, suddenly passed away. After six months, thirty of them had died and around that time, Langlifr moved to a larger workshop with a separate storage area.

Rumours started circulating that Calix Bloodshard had made some sort of deal with the evil dragon Hefnd and was paying for it with the lives of his relatives. Others said that he was poisoning them, while some thought that they had uncovered something in the mine which had cursed the family and which had subsequently been re-buried in the hope of breaking the curse. Sometimes Langlifr was mentioned, although those rumours tended to be amongst the more outlandish and least convincing, which she found highly entertaining. She often heard such rumours as she enjoyed her ale at the inn near her home, but even though people knew who she was, there never seemed to be any suspicion directed towards her. Calix Bloodshard was not a popular person and it seemed that people found it easier to believe that he would have made a pact with an infernal dragon than that he had consulted a witch.

She continued to travel and seek the Instrument and Hefnd's Cup, whilst simultaneously learning all she could about the properties of Death's Fingers and deepening her understanding of its place in the ritual.

Many years passed and Langlifr had just returned home from a hugely unsuccessful voyage to the depths of the Hheserakhian desert on the trail of the Instrument. Depressed and frustrated, she headed to the inn with her papers and sat at her usual table, a flagon of ale by her side. The innkeeper was chatting with a couple of Fireforged, who were sitting by the hearth, their scarlet scales shimmering in the firelight. They were special envoys who had travelled from one of the islands off the Hheserakhian coast to represent their dragon kin at the Imperial Court. Langlifr was toying with her ale and cheering herself up by thinking up ways to acquire a Fireforged claw, when the innkeeper's words caught her attention.

Like many innkeepers, this one loved a good gossip. He knew everything about everyone and thought nothing of sharing that information with anyone who entered his establishment, whether they were interested or not. The Fireforged seemed to be listening intently, Langlifr noted, although it was notoriously difficult to read dragons' expressions.

"Well, of course I know the story of Calix Bloodshard," the innkeeper said. He settled himself against the bar and folded his arms. "It's well-known in these parts. Made a pact with Hefnd, so it's said."

"Is that so?" asked the taller of the Fireforged, leaning forward interestedly. "I heard that he paid off the Assassins' Guild and they've been picking off his family one by one."

"I've heard that, too," admitted the innkeeper. "Truth is that no one really knows what happened. All we know is that he did something seventy years ago and it cursed his family. Two hundred and eighty-seven of them, all dead. The oldest member of Clan Bloodshard now is just seventy years old. Just think of it. A Clan Elder at seventy! Unheard of!"

"What became of Bloodshard himself?" asked the other Fireforged curiously.

"Well, that's the strange thing," said the innkeeper, conspiratorially. "There was a bit of a mystery after his death. He'd lost two hundred and eighty-seven relatives, a lot of them less than a hundred years old, which is almost unheard of for dwarves. By the time two hundred and fifty of them were gone, Bloodshard had gone a little...well, peculiar. He kept going on about some ring of his, a blood ruby which he had inherited from his father and wore constantly, day and night. Apparently, what was happening to his family was connected to the ring and he had been tricked, but he could never explain how he had been tricked, or who by. He would try, but the words wouldn't come. Anyway, after the two hundred and eighty-seventh death, Bloodshard sought help at the Temple of the Great Bál. The High Priest became extremely alarmed while they were talking and afterwards, he went a bit odd, too. In the end, they had to send him off to the monastery and get a new priest."

"So what was the mystery?" asked the taller Fireforged.

"Some say that Bloodshard just died one day, but others think that it was something to do with the ruby ring. One woman I talked to a while back thought that Bloodshard had torn it off and thrown it across the room, after which he suddenly passed away. A man who used to work for the family as a guard says he was in the corridor outside Bloodshard's room on the night he died. Bloodshard started screaming something about being strangled by a witch and the guards all rushed in, only to find him thrashing about on the bed, having a one-sided argument with the ruby ring. Whatever happened, after he died, he was laid in state in the temple courtyard, as is usually the case for those who donate generously," the innkeeper said. He leaned forward over the bar and the Fireforged leaned towards him, eager to catch his words. He lowered his voice and said, "His body disappeared for a few hours and when it was returned, his ruby ring had vanished!"

"Surely that was just despicable grave robbers?" asked the other Fireforged. "Some people have no respect for the dead."

"No one was ever caught. No one ever admitted to having done it. The family didn't make much of a fuss – it was almost like they were just going through the motions of what was expected of them. They were too busy enjoying their inheritance, especially as the unusual deaths stopped after Bloodshard went. But I heard that after the two hundred and eighty-seventh death, Bloodshard started really obsessing over that ruby ring. I'm not surprised that, of all the jewels he was wearing when they laid him out, that was the one that would be stolen. It was so well-known around here. They say it's cursed and if you find it, it will give you eternal life, but bring you nothing but bad luck. Definitely not one to go looking for, in my humble opinion, but some people are only interested in money and that ring would have been worth a fortune."

The Fireforged thanked the innkeeper and began talking to each other in their own language, their voices low. Langlifr smiled. It really had worked out perfectly. Bloodshard had outlived his annoying relatives, just as he had wanted. She had her supply of Death's Fingers and her search for the last two elements of the ritual was still ongoing. She wondered where the ruby ring was. It would be interesting to see what happened to the next person who tried it on…

The ruby ring never reappeared and, to this day, no one has seen it. Many have tried to track it down, but without success. Maybe that is just as well. Some things should remain lost for all time.

And as for Langlifr, she also vanished, along with her papers. Some claim to have seen her at night, flitting between the houses with a bulging bag. Hefnd's Cup is still a legend and the Instrument remains as mysterious as ever, so hopefully, the world is safe from Langlifr's evil schemes for a while yet.

The Bride Stone

Once upon a time, in the southernmost reaches of the Hheserakhian Empire, there lived a maiden named Anora, whose father, Frederic, was a senior politician in the local government. He assisted the province's overlord in the day-to-day management of the land, dealing mainly with trade. The overlord, Jabir, was half-human and half-troll, which terrified some people and they refused to deal with him, leaving Anora's father to undertake transactions in his place. Jabir was well-known for his foul temper and unsavoury habits, so it was no surprise to anyone that he was unwed, in spite of his wealth and his enviable social position. He had a vast, beautiful house in a sprawling estate on the outskirts of Fairhaven, the province's largest port city. Anora and her parents lived not far away in a more modest house with a large landscaped garden.

Of course, over time, seeing Anora at functions and, occasionally, walking along while he passed in his carriage, Jabir couldn't help noticing that she had grown into a charming and intelligent young woman, whose love of books was well-known. She was a skilled archer and, like her mother, Catalina, an expert horsewoman who lit up any room she walked into. As the months passed, he realised that he was in love with her and began watching her closely when they happened to meet, looking for any sign that she might return his affection. However, he was disappointed, for Anora treated him no differently than any other man she encountered at dinners or dances, although he noticed that she spent far longer with people who practised archery, talking intently and animatedly, her eyes sparkling with enthusiasm. It made him want her all the more, for her vitality was infectious and it inspired him.

He decided to broach the subject with Frederic, to see if he had any suggestions on the best way to win his daughter's heart. However, Frederic was less than enthusiastic about the prospect.

"I'm afraid my daughter has indicated that she has feelings for someone else," Frederic said carefully, wary of triggering his employer's ire.

Jabir stared at him in disbelief. "Who?" he demanded. "I have never once seen her pay particular attention to any one individual. Who is this man?"

Frederic shook his head. "I cannot say, for neither of them has expressed their feelings to the other, as far as I am aware, and it would be wrong of me to betray her trust in such a manner."

Jabir snorted angrily and swiped at a pile of papers on the edge of his desk, sending them scattering onto the floor, then stormed out of the room, muttering darkly to himself. Frederic, who was well-used to his employer's foul temper, knelt down and started gathering the papers, a little frown of concern clouding his usually unflappable expression. He had had no idea how Jabir felt about Anora, but while he might admire his employer's negotiating skills and his ability to juggle several vastly complicated transactions at once, he was not particularly keen to see his daughter involved with such a man. He knew how cruel Jabir could be, how he enjoyed petty torments and how he could destroy people's confidence with a few harsh words. Yes, he was articulate, extremely well-read and enjoyed great wealth, but he was not, deep down, a good person and Frederic could not even begin to contemplate any sort of relationship between his daughter and Jabir.

Weeks passed and Jabir did not bring the subject up again, so Frederic guessed that he had taken the hint and moved on. He was disappointed that neither Anora nor Kaden, her young man, had been brave enough to express their feelings to each other. There had been a couple of dinners they had all attended, but the young people had been seated at opposite ends of the table and had had no opportunity to speak with each other. After the meal itself, when the dancing had begun, Frederic had watched them closely, but although a couple of looks were exchanged, it was no more than most of the other men were doing, for Anora, in a gown of red silk, looked truly captivating. She danced with everyone who asked her and Frederic found himself feeling mildly irritated that Kaden was not one of them.

A week or two afterwards, Frederic was standing by his open office window, looking out over the city to the sea beyond. It was a bright, glorious day and the sea was sparkling in the sunlight. Gulls swooped overhead and he could hear traders in the market in the square below as they called out to customers and exchanged banter with each other. He took another draught of his ale and sighed. Although Anora had said nothing more about Kaden, he could tell that she was saddened at his lack of response. As a concerned father, his first instinct was to rush over to the lad's house and talk some sense into him, but he knew that Anora would never forgive him for interfering in such a way. She was a strong woman and more than capable of managing her own life, as her mother kept reminding him. He just felt so helpless, which was something he was not used to and it did not sit comfortably.

He sighed again, cast one last glance out over the view and then turned back to his desk. Settling himself in his chair, he threw himself into his work in an effort to distract himself. However, not long afterwards, his assistant, an extremely efficient half-elf named Arthin, knocked on the door and announced that Anora was outside and wondered if he had time to speak with her.

It was extremely unusual for her to come to his office and he was immediately concerned. Urging his assistant to show her in straight away, he got up and headed to the door, meeting her on the threshold. She threw herself into his arms and began to weep.

This was so unexpected and so out of character for her that, at first, Frederic had no idea what to do. He led her to the sofa and made her comfortable, then hurried to Arthin to ask for wine.

He sat down next to Anora, holding her until her sobs began to subside. Arthin brought in some wine on a tray, which he placed on a low table next to the sofa, then left discreetly, closing the door quietly behind him.

"Oh, Father," began Anora, her voice trembling, "I don't know what to do! I have got myself into a terrible mess and

I am afraid that I cannot undo what has been set in motion!"

Alarmed, Frederic exclaimed, "Why? What on earth has happened?"

Anora closed her eyes for a moment, an expression of anguish on her face. "I have been foolish," she said in a low voice. "I thought that I could handle it, but…"

"Daughter, you are not making any sense," Frederic said anxiously. "Please – start at the beginning. I have no idea what you are talking about. Handle what?"

She sighed heavily and took a deep draught from the glass he handed her. A moment or two later, she began to explain.

Some weeks before, she had plucked up the courage to speak to Kaden and had called at his house to see him, but he had behaved very strangely. He seemed terrified that she was on the doorstep and had quickly bustled her inside, as though he didn't want anyone to see. Puzzled, she had allowed herself to be ushered into a small sitting room at the rear of the house, which looked out onto the garden. This was a significant slight, for etiquette dictated that guests were always directed to the main reception room at the front of the house, unless there was a personal connection which required less formality. As Anora and Kaden did not yet have such a connection, she was surprised and rather offended, although she decided to hold her tongue and see what happened.

The encounter did not go well. Kaden was extremely nervous and hovered by the window, repeatedly looking out into the garden as though he was being watched. Anora steered the conversation as best she could, but his demeanour made her reluctant to tell him of her feelings, for she was now somewhat confused and did not want to look foolish.

Eventually, after he had glanced out into the garden for what seemed like the hundredth time, Anora had been unable to control her temper. "For the love of Bál, Kaden, what on earth is wrong with you today? Are you embarrassed to be seen with me? Is this why you have insulted me so?"

He turned horrified eyes to her. "I would never insult you, Anora, never! I...I am sorry – I didn't know what else to do when I saw you there." He trailed off weakly as her indignation rose.

"Well, I suggest that you read up on etiquette," she said tartly. "Although I have no doubt that you are perfectly aware of what you have done –"

He cut her off. "It was to protect you," he said quickly. "I have to protect you. You shouldn't be here. It isn't safe."

She blinked. "Not safe? How?"

Kaden flicked his eyes towards the garden again, then crossed the room and knelt beside her, grasping her hand. "Please forgive me. I wanted to tell you how I feel about you, but just as I thought I was finally ready to speak to you, he told me to leave you alone."

"My father?" Anora was bewildered.

"No," he said quietly. "It was Jabir."

Her mouth fell open and her eyes widened. "Jabir? Jabir told you to leave me alone? Why on earth would he –"

She broke off as the realisation hit her. "No. Please, no. Tell me that he doesn't …" Kaden's face fell and Anora stared in shock. "What did he say?" she whispered.

Kaden bit his lip and let out a long breath. "He cornered me at the last dinner we were at. I was intending to ask you to dance, but as I was making my way around the room to you, he appeared at my side and hustled me into one of the anterooms. He told me that he had been watching me and knew that I was interested in you. He…warned me off."

She narrowed her eyes. "How exactly?" she asked pointedly. "I have never seen you look so terrified. Am I in some kind of danger? Are you?" She gasped as a thought occurred to her. "Have I put you in danger by coming here?"

He shifted uncomfortably and looked away. Horrified, she leapt to her feet. "I have to go," she said. "Write to me instead, until this is dealt with. And it will be dealt with," she added firmly. "How dare he, the monster! Does he think this is the way to win my affection? Bullying and threatening people?"

Kaden caught her arm and gently swung her around to face him. "I don't think he cares about winning your affection," he said quietly. "You know him better than I do and even I know that if he wants something, he just takes it, regardless."

She set her lips. "I will deal with this, Kaden," she said firmly. "I will."

"I will write to you," he said, then tilted her head back and kissed her softly before releasing her. She hurried to the door and slipped out, her footsteps ringing out on the tiled floor as she ran down the hall. He heard the front door open and close and suddenly, the house felt very empty indeed.

Anora had tried to speak to Jabir, but found it difficult to do so without her father's knowledge. Eventually, she managed to catch him outside his office as he got out of his carriage. He greeted her with delight and escorted her inside with great ceremony. She waited until after his assistant had served them drinks before explaining the reason for her visit.

He had taken it badly. He was a powerful man, unused to being denied something he wanted, particularly something he wanted as badly as Anora. She stood her ground, however, refusing to be intimidated by him. He ended by making a veiled threat which she had scoffed at before she left, closing the door firmly behind her. Nothing more had happened to either herself or Kaden and she dared to hope that Jabir had sensibly decided to give up on a lost cause.

However, she noticed that she was being followed every time she left the house, usually by one of Jabir's servants. The man never approached her or did anything in the least threatening, but his presence was unnerving. She tried ignoring him and going about her usual business, but found that she was distracted and easily startled every time she went out. She stumbled more than usual and tended to forget what she needed to buy. She tried to combat this by writing lists, but increasingly, she would leave them on the hall table and forget to pick them up. On one occasion, she had become so frustrated that she had doubled back on herself and accosted the man, demanding to know why he was following her. He was startled and clearly not happy that she had managed to get so close without him realising where she was. All he would say was that it was for her own protection, but he refused to say who was employing him or why she should need protection. She had confirmed with Kaden that the man had no connection to him or his family, so it had to be another of Jabir's machinations. After that, she had tried hard to focus on her errands and to ignore her shadow, but she became increasingly distracted and seriously considered whether it would be more sensible to stay at home and send a servant in her place. Something inside her rebelled at the thought of being trapped in her own home by Jabir's bullying tactics, so she had maintained her usual routine as best she could.

Earlier that day, however, she had almost been run over by a cart after suddenly finding herself in the middle of a busy road and it was at that point that she knew she had to confide in her father.

Frederic listened to her story in horror, his fury rising in his throat. "Go home," he said quietly. "We will deal with this together. I have some ideas and some favours I can call in. I will send out some messages today. Go home and rest. You look exhausted."

He hugged her and took her to the front of the building, where he hailed a carriage to take her home. Returning to his office, he quickly wrote several short letters and then asked his assistant to have them sent as soon as possible. Arthin assured him that he would take care of it immediately and, after donning his cloak and hat and buckling on his sword, he headed off, leaving Frederic torn between challenging Jabir and pretending that he was unaware of what had occurred. He eventually decided on the latter. He had no intention of working for Jabir any longer than was absolutely necessary, so he would need to secure another job before doing anything rash. He only hoped that he could protect Anora in the meantime and prayed to the Great Bál that his contacts would reply promptly before anything else happened.

Once she arrived home and paid the carriage driver, Anora went straight to her room and lay down, falling immediately into a deep and dreamless sleep. She awoke a couple of hours later feeling slightly more refreshed and determined to take action. Kaden had told her about a sorcerer named Apwyn, who lived on the edge of the city and who was known for his remarkable magical ability. He felt sure that Apwyn was the answer to all their difficulties and had urged her to go and see him. Anora had resisted. She herself had no magical ability and was wary of involving powers that she did not understand and over which she had no control. However, as she lay curled up in bed, turning things over in her mind, she knew that she had to at least go and speak with Apwyn. Kaden might be right about him.

She checked the clock on her mantelpiece and saw that there was still a couple of hours before her father arrived home. She rang for Jenet, her maid, and asked to borrow one of her dresses so that she could leave the house undetected. Jenet thought it was an excellent idea and ran off at once, returning a few minutes later with a dress, a cloak and a pair of shoes. Anora quickly put them on and together, the two of them adjusted the clothes with belts and pins, for Jenet was taller and slightly more heavily built than Anora. Finally, when they were both happy, Jenet took the pins from Anora's hair and brushed it out, then styled it so it looked identical to her own. Luckily, their colouring was very similar, so at a glance, Anora would easily pass for the maid.

"If that awful man is hanging around looking out for you, madam, he won't pay any attention to a maid," Jenet pointed out as she wrapped the cloak around Anora and fastened it in place. "If you take my basket, it will look like you're going out on an errand." She stood back and regarded her mistress thoughtfully, then let out a delighted laugh. "Why, madam, you look just like my twin!"

Anora thanked her and cautioned her to say nothing, for, if the ruse worked and she managed to evade Jabir's man, she would be able to use the disguise again. She also instructed Jenet to stay out of sight until her return, for if the man was watching the house and spotted her through a window, the game would be up. Jenet agreed and went downstairs to tell Mrs Merryheart the housekeeper and swear her to secrecy. Mrs Merryheart pursed her lips, concerned, but conceded that the young mistress was sensible to take such precautions and suggested that Jenet spent the next couple of hours working in the laundry out of sight until the young mistress returned.

Anora picked up Jenet's basket and hooked it over her arm as she had seen the maid do, then left through the servants' door, which opened into a lane at the side of the house and ended at a heavy iron gate, beyond which was the street. She made her way along the lane with some trepidation, knowing that her shadow would be there somewhere, lounging against a wall, or under a tree, watching. As she approached the gate and opened the latch, she spotted him and almost froze. He was standing on the pavement opposite the house, pretending to read a newspaper. No matter whether she turned left or right at the end of the lane, she would have to pass him, for he was almost directly in front of her.

Her hand shook as she fumbled with the latch, but she took a deep breath and continued on, turning left at the end of the lane and heading away from the house. Her heart skipped as she realised that Jenet had been right. He was so intent on watching the front door that it never occurred to him that she might use another. She might as well have been invisible.

With a new spring in her step, she headed straight for Apwyn's isolated house near the river on the very edge of the city. He had a beautiful herb garden and she paused to admire it before going to the door and knocking.

He answered a moment later. He was tall and austere, yet his eyes were kind when he invited her in. She explained the difficulty she was in and asked if there was anything he could do to stop Jabir being interested in her, perhaps by casting a spell that made her look incredibly ugly to him, or by giving him a potion that made him instantly forget her.

The sorcerer listened attentively and when she had run out of suggestions, he smiled and went to put a kettle of water on the fire.

"I think we both need a soothing drink," he said. "You have clearly suffered a great deal lately and there is something I can do to help you, although it is costly."

"I have money," she said simply.

He nodded, then excused himself and went to the herb garden, where he took leaves from several plants and placed them in the kettle. "These are calming and fortifying," he explained. "I will give you some to take home, for I think they will help you greatly."

He asked her several questions about Jabir's personality and habits, then fell into a silent contemplation until the kettle started to steam. He rose and strained the fragrant liquid into two goblets and passed one to Anora, who lifted it to her nose and breathed in the exquisite aroma while she waited for the liquid to cool. Apwyn went to a cupboard, opened the door and perused the contents, stroking his long, iron grey beard. He reached in and took out a small glass vial, looked at it carefully, then replaced it and selected another. He did this a few times, muttering under his breath. Finally, he took out a small green bottle, uncorked it and sniffed the contents delicately, then replaced the stopper and regarded it thoughtfully for a minute or two. He then turned to a large leather-bound book on a stand next to the cupboard, opened it and flipped through the pages until he found what he was looking for. He spent several minutes reading before closing the book and sitting opposite Anora.

"Take this," he said, holding out the green bottle. "This is a potion which, when drunk, will turn a person to stone."

Anora froze, her hand outstretched towards the bottle. "To stone?" she exclaimed. "I don't want to kill him, just make him leave me alone!"

Apwyn smiled. "You have a beautiful heart, lady," he said. "Do not worry, for there is a way to undo the spell. You must collect your tears in a vial and keep them safe. If you decide one day that the lesson has been learned and the spell can be undone, you must sprinkle the stone with the contents of the vial and its effects will gradually wear off."

Anora considered before accepting the potion. "As long as he won't die and I have a way to reverse the spell, I am happy," she said. "Thank you."

He told her the price, which was less than she had been expecting, and she handed over the coins. He gave her a little glass vial for her tears, then busied himself making up a parcel of herbs. When she thanked him for his care, he smiled and winked at her. "You are disguised as a maid, lady. If you go back with an empty basket, it will look suspicious. This parcel will help you maintain your disguise, as well as restore your spirit."

 He escorted her to the gate and she thanked him again, then bade him farewell and headed home, being careful to go in through the servants' door. Her shadow had moved and was now further down the road, so she was able to get into the house completely undetected.

She had hidden the green potion in her purse, so all the basket contained was the parcel of herbs, which she entrusted to the cook with instructions on how to prepare the infusion. She hurried to her room, where Jenet was waiting to help her into her own clothes. Just as she was slipping on her shoes, she heard her father returning home.

"That was good timing, madam," said Jenet with a conspiratorial smile. "I hope you found everything you needed."

"Yes, I did, thank you," replied Anora, returning the smile. She headed downstairs to see her parents, wondering how she would be able to administer the potion without being detected.

Her chance came unexpectedly shortly afterwards. Jabir and Frederic had just concluded a complex trade deal with an envoy from Qalarmah, one of the lands across the ocean to the east of the Empire. The deal would bring a considerable amount of new money into the province and a significant number of new jobs would be created at the docks, which was a boon for the city. Jabir decided to throw a party at his estate to celebrate and, of course, Anora was on the guest list. She was apprehensive about going, especially after her father announced the news about the trade deal. Suddenly the whole situation seemed harsh, especially as Jabir had not contacted her or mentioned her to her father in recent days. Nothing seemed to have come of his veiled threat to her, either, but every time she glanced out of a window or left the house and saw Jabir's man watching her every move, she was reminded of why the potion had become necessary in the first place.

After agonising over the party for the better part of a week, Anora finally decided that she would go. She experimented with the green bottle and found that it sat beautifully in the gathered sleeve of her dark blue evening gown. She had been collecting her tears in the little glass vial, which she wore on a chain around her neck, so she would at least be able to reverse the spell should she need to. Of course, she thought ruefully, that would entirely depend on whether it was appropriate to administer the potion, and whether she would manage to do so in the first place. That was a problem she would have to overcome on the night, once she had had a chance to judge the situation.

The party started well. Jabir was extremely jovial and behaved much better than he usually did. It was unfortunate that alcohol did not mix well with his troll blood, bringing out his worst traits. Anora began to relax, for he had paid her no attention whatsoever, except when he politely greeted her at the door. She watched him out of the corner of her eye for a while, but he wasn't even so much as glancing in her direction. He was with a crowd of richly dressed men from the Merchants' Guild, towering over them and laughing heartily. She saw her parents on the far side of the room, talking with one of the senior mercers and the head of the Apothecaries' Guild. Catching her father's eye, she flashed him a quick smile, before turning to accept an offer to dance. Her partner, an apprentice armourer named Tomas, was an excellent dancer and she hoped that he would ask her for another dance. As she whirled around, her skirts billowing, she suddenly caught a glimpse of Jabir, standing alone at the edge of the dance floor, staring at her. She let out a little cry, causing Tomas some concern, as he thought she had hurt herself. He began to escort her from the dance floor, but she begged him to stay so they could finish the dance. She had no desire to be anywhere near Jabir and was hoping that by the time the dance ended, he would have been distracted by another group of people, so she could disappear into the crowd without him noticing her.

The dance ended and she thanked Tomas, who escorted her to the bar and bought her a drink, happy to be in her company for a little longer. They chatted for a while about the trade deal and the benefits it would bring to the city, particularly to his trade, then he asked her if she would honour him with the next dance, to which she happily agreed.

Just then, the music started and Tomas took her hand to lead her to the dance floor. He had just spun her around and taken her in his arms when Jabir suddenly appeared in front of them. "May I cut in?" he asked formally.

Her partner frowned slightly, but clearly felt that he could not refuse his host, so he nodded and mutely handed Anora to Jabir and retreated to the edge of the dance floor with a sullen expression on his face. A couple of men next to him, who had witnessed the exchange, laughed and clapped him on the back, consoling him. Anora, feeling trapped, briefly considered refusing, but decided that it was probably the safest place to test the waters with regard to Jabir's feelings towards her. There was a room full of people around them that she could call on for help if she needed it.

Jabir was not an accomplished dancer. Anora felt that he was carrying her more than dancing with her, for her feet scarcely touched the ground. He was such a large man – tall and immensely strong because of his troll blood. His arm around her waist was rock hard and the huge hand clasping hers felt like a vice.

For a while, she didn't know what to say, so they moved around in silence. Eventually, Jabir looked down at her and smiled a calculating, cruel smile. He stank of alcohol.

"You're looking particularly beautiful tonight," he said.

"Thank you," she replied shortly.

"That dress suits you well."

"Thank you."

They danced in silence again for a while.

"I need a drink," he said suddenly. "I have some beautiful wine in my office. Come and try some."

"No, thank you," she said.

"Why not?" he asked, irritably. "What is wrong with you? I invite you to my house and offer you hospitality and you throw it back in my face! You will come and have a drink with me right now, or your father will no longer have work in my office."

She struggled against his grip, but it was like fighting with a building. "How dare you try to control me like this," she snapped. "You have had me watched and followed for weeks, you have bullied and intimidated people I care about and now this? Let me go!"

She struggled against his arm, glancing left and right, hoping to find her father or Tomas. In response, Jabir lifted her off her feet and started carrying her from the dance floor. "Let me go!" she cried furiously. "Let me go at once!"

"I need a drink and you're going to have one with me," he informed her. "Stop fighting me and enjoy my hospitality."

"Let her go, Jabir," her father's voice rang out authoritatively as he approached them. "This has gone far enough. My daughter is not interested in you and I will not stand by and watch you treat her in this way."

Jabir stopped and turned to face Frederic, still holding Anora, who was struggling for all she was worth. They were right in front of the orchestra and some of the musicians were becoming distracted by the sight of the host holding a clearly distressed young woman while an older man berated him. The music began to peter out and the dancers, puzzled, slowed their steps and looked around to see what had happened. As soon as people spotted Anora's struggles and saw the expressions on Jabir's and Frederic's faces, they began to step in to ask what was going on. Tomas hurried over and tried to forcibly remove Jabir's arm from around Anora's waist, but the man simply swatted him aside as though he were a fly. He flew backwards a few feet, crashing into six or seven of the onlookers, who also fell in a tangle of limbs and skirts.

"Enough!" snapped Frederic, finally losing his temper. "This is unbecoming! Release my daughter this instant!"

The room collectively held its breath as everyone watched to see what Jabir would do. He was clearly already drunk.

Jabir looked around at the sea of faces staring back at him, some horrified, some angry, some simply enjoying the spectacle as they waited for his next move. He looked down at Anora's furious face as she struggled, then released his grip and pushed her backwards, none too gently, towards Tomas. She staggered and fell as her skirts tangled around her legs. As she landed, she felt the green bottle shoot out of her right sleeve. It slid across her collarbone and came to rest in the crook of her left arm as she lay there, stunned. Several people hurried forward to help her, but stopped when Jabir let out a roar. He had spotted the bottle.

"What have we here?" he demanded.

Anora froze, unable to answer at first. Eventually, she whispered, "Nothing. It's nothing."

She grabbed the bottle and began scrambling backwards away from him. A few people began shouting at Jabir to leave her alone and others ran forward to help her to her feet. She stuffed the bottle back into her sleeve, still backing away towards the door. Her father was nose to nose with Jabir, looking more furious than she had ever known. She could hear her mother's voice calling to her, but couldn't find her in the sea of concerned faces. She just kept backing towards the door, desperate to get away.

Jabir roared again and sent Frederic hurtling backwards across the room. Anora screamed in terror, then turned and fled, hardly knowing where she was going. She ran down the hall towards the front door, hearing Jabir's footsteps as he charged after her, yelling, "What's in the bottle, Anora? What is it?"

Her fear drove her onwards, out of the front door, down the steps and onto the drive. She could hear other footsteps now, as the party-goers, realising that something dreadful was happening, all swarmed out of the ballroom after Jabir, some shouting at him to stop and others calling to her, some telling her to run and others urging her to hide. She risked a glance behind her and stifled a scream as she realised how close Jabir was. His strength and long legs enabled him to cover the ground between them extremely quickly and she knew it was a matter of moments before he caught her. She thought she heard her father's voice in the chaos, but her head was spinning in terror and her heart was pounding so loudly that all she heard was a cacophony of voices that made her ears ring painfully. She ran as fast as she could towards the end of the drive, hoping that she could make it along the road, where there might be a carriage.

All of a sudden, Jabir let out the loudest, most fearsome roar she had ever heard and the noise from the partygoers stopped abruptly. Some of the women screamed in fear, and one or two men cried out as Jabir turned and rounded on them. "Stay away from me!" he roared. "Stay back, or you will feel my wrath! This is between her and me. It's nothing to do with any of you. Do you hear me? It's none of your business! Now get back inside MY house and carry on

81

drinking MY wine and eating MY food, you worthless, ungrateful worms. If any of you come just one step closer, you will regret it for the rest of your incredibly short life!"

He flexed his hands as he spoke, his knuckles popping. Some of the guests turned and fled back inside, while some remained frozen to the spot in horror, wondering what on earth this terrible man was going to do next. Anora had almost reached the end of the drive and the guests found themselves desperately hoping that a cart would drive past and pick her up.

Jabir thundered down the drive towards the gate. Anora had reached it now and was running along the road. There were no carts in sight, but it was late and the road was dark, so it was unlikely that there would be very many people driving out at that hour.

She was tiring. Jabir's estate was a mile or two from the edge of the city and she knew that she had neither the strength nor the stamina to make it that far. All she could do was hide somewhere, but she was running along a straight section of road, with Jabir not far behind her. If she left the road now, he would easily spot her.

She could hear him grunting as he pounded after her and realised that he was even closer than she had thought. She pushed herself as hard as she could, but she knew that she was slowing, not speeding up...and then he grabbed her shoulder and lifted her off her feet for a horrible, endless moment, before he slowed down and stopped, still holding on to her as she struggled and cried in terror.

"What is in that bottle?" he demanded, grabbing her sleeve and yanking it so that the fabric ripped. She managed to catch the bottle before it fell and he let go of her shoulder to try to take it from her. "What is it? Tell me!"

She could only shake her head, her tears blinding her and her sobs catching in her throat. He advanced on her as she retreated. "Tell me," he repeated. "Tell me, or your life won't be worth living! I will send people to hound your every move. Nothing you do will be a secret to me. I will know everything about you. Everything. Every single day for the rest of your life. Tell me!"

She finally found her voice. "Why are you doing this to me?" she sobbed.

He snorted. "Why? Because you refused me without reason. I could have given you anything you wanted. Yet you refused me."

She stared at him. "I owed you nothing," she said wretchedly. "Please, please, just leave me alone. That is all I want."

"And I want to know what is in the bottle, Anora," he said menacingly, taking a step towards her. "If you don't tell me, I will personally see to it that your father ends up on the street. No matter where he goes in the world, he will never be able to get a position. Not even as a street sweeper! Is that what you want? Is it?"

She stared at him in disbelief, unable to comprehend how someone could be so cruel and yet wonder why he had been rejected. For a moment, she couldn't quite believe what she had just heard. As she stood there staring at him, his words sank in and she knew without a shadow of doubt that he meant every single one of them.

It was then that she knew what she had to do.

"The green bottle contains a headache remedy," she said in a quavering voice. "I have been suffering with them a lot lately."

"Prove it," he said pointedly.

"What?"

"Prove that it is a headache remedy," he said nastily. "Drink it."

At that moment, everything changed. She saw her life stretching out before her, filled with fear and paranoia, her every move being dogged by Jabir and his uncaring, unfeeling henchmen. She saw her father and mother begging on the streets. She saw herself as the unwilling bride of the evil creature in front of her, forced to use her body as currency to buy back her parents' home and her father's livelihood. No matter what she did, Jabir would always be there at her back and she would never know a moment's peace.

Slowly, she uncorked the bottle and raised it to her lips.

He watched as she tilted the bottle and swallowed the concoction within, then dropped the bottle at her feet and stared at him.

He uttered a short laugh and shook his head. "There," he said, "that wasn't difficult, was it? So much fuss over a simple instruction! Now let's go and have that drink." As he spoke, he caught hold of her shoulder again and started dragging her back along the road. She wept quietly as he pulled her along, but said nothing.

After a minute or two, Jabir stopped, for Anora seemed to be getting increasingly heavy and he was having difficulty in moving her. He glanced back to see what she was doing, but she was simply standing there, staring at him with huge, accusing, baleful eyes, which rather unnerved him. He took hold of her again and pulled, but she didn't move and he staggered backwards, almost losing his footing. He stared at her in confusion until she glanced down at her feet. Following her gaze, his eyes widened in shock, for her gown was no longer a beautiful, rich blue, but now resembled granite, as though it had turned to stone. He reached out uncomprehendingly to touch the fabric, but jerked his hand away in horror when his fingers met cold, hard rock. Even as he watched, he could see the stone creeping upwards towards her waist. Terrified, he met her gaze. She was utterly motionless, her hands folded beneath her chin as her eyes swivelled to look at him.

"What have I done?" he whispered hoarsely. "What have I done?"

Her eyes accused him and he found that he could not look away. He threw himself at her feet and wept as the stone crept ever higher. As it reached her arms, he began apologising repeatedly, tears running down his face.

"Do not waste your words, Jabir," she said in a voice as hard as the stone that was enveloping her. "Look on your handiwork and remember this moment, for hereafter, it is

I who will hound your every waking moment. Whenever you see the blue of the sky, you will remember my gown. Whenever you see a rock, or a mountain, or a pebble, or a stone building, you will think of me. Whenever you see a green bottle, you will remember the moment you destroyed my life. I repay you by cursing and destroying your life, and the lives of anyone who tries to hurt me. I curse you, Jabir of the Sakura Mountain trolls!"

Stunned and almost speechless with fright, Jabir begged her to stop what she was doing, but the stone had reached her neck and a moment later, it was all over.

After an hour or so, a few of the braver partygoers found him lying at the base of a standing stone which had suddenly appeared in the middle of the road. They thought at first that he had placed it there himself, but when some of the men went to move it out of the way, they realised that it was part of the ground and could not be moved. As they stood staring at it in confusion, one of the women said quietly, "I travelled along this road to get to the party. There was no stone here then."

"I use this road a lot," one of the men said to her. "You're right. This stone wasn't here before. What has he done?"

One of the women began to sob and another said firmly, "He cannot continue to hold office after this."

Several of them agreed with her. They all stood staring at the stone, wondering how they were going to break the news to Frederic and Catalina.

Jabir was immediately removed from office and handed control of the province to Frederic, who threw himself into the role with a grim determination and intensity which his staff found unnerving. They all believed that he had returned to work far too soon after the tragedy, but he refused to listen to them, insisting that the work helped him to cope. Initially, they tiptoed around him as if on eggshells, until he lost his temper. His calm demeanour was gone forever, replaced with a fury almost equal to that of his predecessor. He governed well, but he proved to be a hard man. His empathy was gone and all that remained was a grieving empty shell.

Jabir quickly became obsessed with finding someone who could break the spell. He started by visiting Apwyn, but found that the sorcerer was travelling and would not be back for some time, so instead, he sent messages to every contact he had throughout the Empire and beyond, asking for help. Unfortunately, when the replies started arriving, they were not what he was hoping for. No one had heard of any wizard, sorcerer or witch who had cast such a spell. Months passed and Jabir gave up all hope of ever restoring Anora to life. He was known ever after as the monster who had hounded a girl to her death and he remained friendless and alone for the rest of his days.

After a couple of years had gone by, Apwyn returned from his travels. He passed Jabir's estate on his way back home and knew he was almost there, for the estate had long been a landmark for travellers, letting them know that they were almost at the city.

As he walked, he came across a strange sight. Ahead of him, in the middle of the road, there was an odd standing stone. It was completely out of place and he knew that it had not been there when he left, yet as he approached and looked at it curiously, he could see that it was protruding from the ground. He looked around in confusion, for the road had been dug out on one side so that carts could still pass around the stone. He laid his hand on it and was shocked to find that it felt warm to the touch. He pursed his lips as he remembered the young woman to whom he had given the potion. Bending down, he put his ear to the stone and, sure enough, he could just make out a very faint heartbeat.

As he straightened, he saw Jabir approaching from the other direction, carrying a bag from which protruded a number of scrolls. Jabir frowned when he saw Apwyn, but as he neared, he realised who it was. "Sorcerer!" he exclaimed, hurrying forward. "You have returned at last."

"Aye," replied Apwyn, still studying the stone.

"I would pick your brain, sorcerer, if I may," Jabir began.

Apwyn raised an eyebrow, wondering what Jabir wanted. "You may."

Jabir told him what had happened with Anora and the potion – although it was a heavily edited version. As he spoke, Apwyn realised that this must be the man who Anora had been trying to rid herself of. Clearly something had gone very wrong.

"I am familiar with this spell," he said mildly. "There is an antidote. Did the young lady have about her person a small glass vial containing a clear liquid?"

Jabir racked his brain, trawling through fractured memories of the traumatic event. "I am not sure," he said finally. "She was wearing a necklace of some sort, I remember that much."

"Did she have a purse?"

Jabir thought again. "No," he said. "No, she didn't. Not that night."

Apwyn nodded thoughtfully. "In order to break the spell, the person administering it must collect some of their tears in a glass vial," he said. "They then have to the power to either end the spell or let it continue. It will continue until such time as they sprinkle their tears onto the stone, at which point the victim is restored to life."

Jabir eyed him narrowly. "I see," he said. "I thank you for your help, sorcerer."

Apwyn nodded and set off on his way again. After he had gone a short distance, Jabir called out, "It is strange, sorcerer, is it not, that I have sent enquiries throughout the world to find a way to break this spell and not a single person had even heard of it. Yet the one person who knows it in detail just happens to live in the same city as myself. Quite the coincidence, don't you think?"

Apwyn turned back and regarded him coolly. "Indeed," he acknowledged. "Funny things, coincidences. Good luck in tracking down the antidote."

Jabir watched him go, then looked at the stone, re-running his memories over and over to see if he could remember a glass vial. Eventually, he gave up and walked to Frederic's house, where he waited for one of the servants to leave on an errand. After a couple of hours, a young maid emerged from the lane at the side of the house and for a moment, he thought Anora had miraculously returned to life, for the maid looked very like her, although a little taller. He hastened to catch up with her as she strode purposefully along the road, a basket hooked over her arm.

Upon seeing him, her eyes widened with fear at first, but then her entire expression darkened to one of hate and anger. "What do you want?" she demanded. "How dare you come here?"

"I am trying to find a way to break the spell," he protested. "I need your help. Did your mistress have a little glass vial with clear liquid in it?"

The maid stared at him before replying slowly, "Yes, she did, but only for a few days before... before she..." She broke off and took a deep breath. "She wore it on a chain around her neck."

His hopes shattered and he simply stared at her as she turned and marched away.

He walked slowly back to the stone and spent a long time examining it. There was an imprint of a hand where her left shoulder had been and he shuddered as he thought of how he had pulled her along the road. He traced the outline of the stone where her arms had been and realised that in between the two ridges, there was a small lump which sat roughly where a pendant might rest. Excited at the thought that this might be the vial, he ran to his house to get some tools, then hastened back to the stone, thinking that it would be relatively easy to chip it off and see if it was still intact inside its stone casing. Positioning his chisel carefully, he struck it once with his hammer, then dropped both as a blood-curdling, ear-splitting scream filled the air. He staggered backwards, clapping his hands to his ears and falling to his knees, unable to think or speak until the all-encompassing noise finally stopped as abruptly as it had started.

From that day, the stone has remained untouched. Jabir never again tried to retrieve the vial and every time he tried to find Apwyn to seek his help, the sorcerer seemed to have vanished. Eventually, Jabir gave up his quest to find an alternative antidote and spent his days drinking and gambling. He lost his entire fortune and his estate had to be broken up and sold off to pay his debts. He wandered around the city as a vagrant for a while, but he had wronged far too many people and was found one day by the harbourmaster, floating face down in the water. He was given a pauper's burial and there was no one to mourn him.

The stone became known as the Bride Stone and became a warning to over-enthusiastic suitors. It stands today at the centre of a crossroads, which had to be designed around it. After Jabir's estate was broken up and sold off, the city naturally began to expand in that direction and the roads had to be widened and improved to cope with the increasing number of goods wagons. One of the road workers started digging at the base of the stone in an attempt to remove it, as it was not in his plans. However, as soon as his shovel broke the soil, the stone emitted a high-pitched scream, the likes of which he had never heard before. The man was haunted for months by the sound of a woman screaming and sobbing in agony and he suffered the most terrible bad luck for years, until his early death. The same thing happened to another worker who also tried to remove the stone. The plans were quickly changed to incorporate the stone and the construction company gave its workers strict orders not to disturb it.

As the years went by, the Bride Stone's reputation grew. Attempting to damage or disturb it is extremely unlucky and usually results in the eventual ruin of the person concerned, who is cursed with bad luck for the rest of their life. Some people claim to have seen the ghost of a young woman pacing their carriage as they neared the crossroads, disappearing once they had passed the stone. There is certainly an odd feeling in the air along that section of the road and many travellers have similar tales to tell when they arrive at the city's inns.

The Sacred Well of the Goddess of Fortune

There are, unsurprisingly, many stories about the founding of the first Temple of the Goddess of Fortune, who has always attracted a large following, both in the Empire and the lands beyond. This is the most popular of the tales.

In the world's early days, when the tragedy of the Benevolent Frodleikr's death was just a few generations past, Bál's creatures began to find deities in trees, rivers, the wind, the ocean, the darkness... anything to which they could link a significant event in their lives. The cult of the Goddess of Fortune was highly inclusive, for she could smile on anyone whether they be king or beggar and, therefore, people flocked to pray and to petition her whenever they needed a little luck.

Over the years, many had laid claim to founding the Goddess's first Temple, usually wealthy citizens who enjoyed letting everyone know just how generous they were and who always made a great show of stopping in the street to give a beggar a few coins. However, according to this tale, the Temple of the Goddess of Fortune was founded by a couple of very unlikely characters.

Silas the ostler and Martyn the farrier were two of the most impious men that ever lived. They were true salt-of-the-earth types, lovable rogues who always had a twinkle in their eye and an endless supply of quips and banter. Both had a great affinity with horses and were skilled in their trades, but they had an equally great affinity with ale and women. Most evenings found them in one of the inns, regaling the drinkers with jokes and bawdy stories. Innkeepers loved them, for they always created a jovial and welcoming atmosphere, they spent a fortune on ale – and encouraged others to do likewise – and there were far fewer brawls to deal with. Any innkeeper seeing the two of them walking into his establishment knew he was in for an easy and profitable night.

It so happened that, one evening, the two friends had met a couple of girls from the next village and had offered to escort them home at the end of the night, expecting to be invited to stay overnight due to the lateness of the hour. However, the young ladies had no intention of inviting two virtual strangers into their home, no matter how charming they were. The two friends found themselves on a dimly-lit street in a deserted village well after midnight, staring at the front door which had just been closed on them.

They exchanged a rueful glance and then burst out laughing. "Ah well," said Martyn with a shrug. "They were good company. I'll probably call on Anna in a day or two."

"You're just thinking about building your empire," Silas teased. "You're only interested in her because she's a leather worker and you could start to offer saddlery services!"

"That's not true!" Martyn protested with a chuckle. "Although I know what services I'd like to offer Anna!"

A window opened above them and Anna looked out, trying unsuccessfully to look annoyed. "If you two don't clear off and stop keeping us and our neighbours awake, the only 'service' of mine you'll experience is my dinner service, as I throw it at your head!" she chided, but even in the near darkness, Martyn could see the twinkle in her eye. He beamed at her and bowed low.

"Then I will wish you goodnight, my lady, and return to my castle to dream of you."

"Drunken fool," said Anna, almost fondly, as she closed the window. A moment later, the light in her room went out.

Silas let out a loud guffaw. "'I will return to my castle and dream of you'?" he repeated. "For the love of Bál, what have you been drinking tonight?"

Martyn smirked. "You're just jealous of my amazing way with words."

"I'm amused by your amazingly wayward words, more like, you clown," Silas retorted. "Come on. We'd best be heading back. I doubt any innkeeper would let us in at this hour, even if I had the money for a room."

They set off, reliving the evening blow by blow and mocking each other's speech, mannerisms, choice of ale and tolerance for alcohol. Their route took them through a thick forest which they both knew relatively well, for it was a favoured meeting place for young people and the two had used it on many occasions to meet with various young ladies of their acquaintance. They had no torches with them, but the path was good and Máni's heart shone brightly in a cloudless sky. It was only after they had gone a short way into the forest that they realised how ill-prepared they were. They could scarcely see their hands in front of their faces, for the canopy overhead was lush and dense. In their usual manner, the friends shrugged and continued on, unperturbed. After all, it wasn't the first time they had been in that situation.

They had been walking for some time when Martyn paused to remove a stone from his shoe. As he shook it out, they both distinctly heard slow, even, heavy footsteps approaching them from the direction of the village behind them.

There were stories, as there often are, of ghosts and spirits haunting the forest, but neither of the friends had ever experienced anything in the least unusual and tended to scoff at such tales. They were very aware, however, that they were somewhat the worse for drink and unarmed. Martyn had his small work knife and Silas had a random hoof pick in his pocket, but both would be useless in a fight. Occasionally, people had been attacked by highwaymen whilst travelling through the forest, and there was at least one band of goblins living somewhere amongst the trees.

Martyn put his shoe on and the two of them continued walking. They could still hear footsteps behind them, louder now, but when they turned to look, they saw nothing and guessed it was probably goblins, which didn't alarm them particularly. Goblins were notorious cowards. Grab a couple and knock their heads together and the whole band would take fright and run away.

Time passed and the footsteps grew louder, yet no matter how often they turned around, there was no one to be seen. They started to feel a little uncomfortable. Silas noticed a stout stick near the path and paused to pick it up. Its weight and solidity were reassuring and he gave it a couple of experimental swings as they walked. Martyn started looking for something similar, but found nothing, so he took his work knife from his trouser pocket and slid it into his jacket instead.

They quickened their pace a little. Every now and then, Martyn wandered from the path in search of a better weapon, but Silas, concerned at how loud the footsteps were becoming, grabbed his sleeve and pulled him back. "Something doesn't feel right," he muttered. "The path here is straight. Surely we should be able to see whose footsteps those are? They sound like they're just behind us."

Martyn opened his mouth to make a smart remark, but then he noticed something just beyond Silas on the other side of the path. He pointed, a frown creasing his brow. "Silas...isn't that the Ghost Tree?"

Silas turned distractedly, painfully aware of what now sounded like two pairs of hobnailed boots right behind him on the empty path. He glanced over to the tree Martyn indicated, then stopped and stared at the familiar landmark. It was rumoured that a young serving girl had hanged herself from the tree after her lover left her at the altar. People often left flowers amongst its roots as an offering in return for protection from robbers as they passed through the forest.

Silas turned wide eyes on Martyn. "We passed the Ghost Tree earlier!" he hissed.

"And we've been following the path the whole time," Martyn whispered back. "What in the name of Bál is going on?"

Suddenly, a loud cough rang out from behind them and they whirled around, peering into the gloom, but seeing no one. Martyn began to get annoyed.

"Who's there?" he shouted. "Show yourself!"

Silence.

The two men stood frozen, straining their ears, but there was nothing to hear. No more coughing, no footsteps. The forest suddenly felt ominous, the atmosphere oppressive and threatening. They both noticed the subtle shift and exchanged a glance before turning and continuing briskly along the path, almost running at times. Neither looked at the Ghost Tree as they passed it.

They had only gone a short distance when, from somewhere ahead of them, there came a ripple of laughter. Both of them started, now thoroughly annoyed and unnerved. Silas hefted his stick and Martyn, having failed to find anything similar, went to the nearest tree, broke off a branch and started stripping it of leaves and twigs. All at once, the air was filled with the sound of laughter and running footsteps. The two men spun around, trying to see who, or what, was making the noise, but there was no one there. As far as they could tell, they were entirely alone.

"Come on," said Silas grimly. He grabbed Martyn's sleeve and started running, trying to ignore the unnerving, high-pitched laughter that surrounded them. It seemed to be travelling along with them, yet they could still see nothing.

All at once, Silas skidded to a halt so abruptly that Martyn almost fell over him. As they staggered together, trying to regain their balance, Silas gripped Martyn's arm and pointed.

They were back at the Ghost Tree.

Now they were both thoroughly afraid and utterly confused. The path was easy to make out, even in the gloom, yet they had somehow gone around in a complete circle.

"It's impossible," said Silas in disbelief. "We didn't leave the path. We would have had to leave the path and double back on ourselves to end up here."

"I don't like this," said Martyn darkly. "There's magic at work here, Silas. Has to be."

"What do we do?" Silas asked. "We've been walking for a very long time. Shouldn't we have reached home by now?"

Martyn started to answer but the words caught in his throat. He stared at Silas as he tried to work out how long they had been in the forest. "Bál's Claws, Silas, you're right," he breathed. "What the hell is happening here?"

"We have two choices," Silas said. "We either continue on, or find somewhere to rest until morning."

Martyn snorted. "I say continue on," he said. "Don't fancy staying here any longer than necessary."

"I'm with you," Silas said fervently. "Come on."

They walked on briskly, disembodied laughter ringing out around them and what sounded like a dozen sets of footsteps behind them – lighter, now, and quicker. Martyn began to mutter under his breath. Silas couldn't quite make out the words, but he was certain that his friend was praying to the Goddess of Fortune. That scared him more than anything, for he had never known Martyn to do such a thing. They walked on, looking all around them and starting at every twig snap and branch creak. All at once, Silas stopped dead.

"I don't believe this," he said hollowly.

They were back at the Ghost Tree.

Before Martyn could say anything in response, they both heard music – a sweet, gentle melody from somewhere up ahead. Hoping the musician was friendly, they immediately headed towards the source of the music, but as they neared it, a dense fog suddenly arose and they soon struggled to make out the path, forced to slow their steps in case they accidentally wandered from it. Martyn stopped and leaned against a tree, wiping his forehead on his sleeve. He glanced down at his aching feet, then let out a yell of fright as he saw the posies and other offerings around him.

The Ghost Tree.

Except it was now on the opposite side of the path.

For a long moment, neither man moved nor spoke. They simply stared in horror as they realised that they were hopelessly lost within some magical loop and they had no idea how to escape from it.

Martyn backed away from the Ghost Tree and stared helplessly at Silas. "What now?" he asked.

Silas frowned as he tried to remember something he had heard once from a traveller who had arrived at the inn in a terrible state after a strange occurrence in the forest. The music was distracting him and he couldn't quite recall the man's story. It was something to do with clothes, he knew that much.

"Pixies!" he exclaimed loudly all of a sudden, snapping his fingers triumphantly. Martyn started violently and shushed him.

"Keep your voice down!" he hissed. "What are you on about?"

"Do you remember that half-man who came into the inn a while ago, talking about ghosts in the forest?" Silas said urgently, lowering his voice. "He was an apprentice miller, I think. Good boots. A bit naïve. You thought he was eyeing Molly up."

Martyn goggled at him for a moment, then his eyes lit up as the memory came back to him. "Him! I remember. He said something about being chased through the forest by a demon hound, didn't he?"

Silas thought for a moment. "Wasn't that Oregrinder, after he had that mushroom from Giles the Rat?"

Something clicked in place in Martyn's head and he grabbed Silas's shoulders, making him drop his stick. "Pixies! You're right. I remember now. That half-man had heard strange music and ended up wandering off the path. I can't remember how he managed to find it again. I know he did something really simple."

"It was something to do with clothes," Silas said. "I wish I could remember what it was."

Martyn screwed his face up and racked his brain. Suddenly he gave a little laugh. "He had to turn his jacket inside out!" he said, "to protect himself against being pixie-led!"

They stared at each other for a moment as the cacophony of footsteps, music and laughter grew louder and louder all around them. A breeze swirled through the trees, sounding louder and more fierce with every passing moment, yet none of the leaves were moving, no branches were swaying or creaking and the undergrowth was still. They felt like they were in the midst of a hurricane. The noise was deafening and any order they had found in their thoughts was lost as they clapped their hands over their ears and stumbled on along the path in what they hoped was the right direction. Once or twice, they started to stray from the path, but thankfully noticed almost straight away and managed to retrace their steps until they found it again.

The noise built to a roar and it was a while before either could focus enough to speak. Martyn managed first. "Turn your jacket inside out!" he shouted above the racket, starting to struggle out of his. Silas followed suit, yanking the sleeves inside out and pulling it back on as quickly as he could. Almost at once, the noise started to fade and he was relieved to find that he could form coherent thoughts again.

Martyn had dropped to one knee as he fumbled with his sleeve. His face was screwed up in pain as the noise became even louder, a thundering that reverberated inside his head and made his teeth ache. Silas grabbed the jacket, pulled the second sleeve inside out and helped his friend put it on. As he did, Martyn began to relax as the noise started fading for him too. He curled into a ball on the ground until the ringing in his ears started to subside. Silas realised he had lost his stick, so he stood next to his friend, fists ready, looking all around him for signs of danger.

It was a while before Martyn felt well enough to sit up and longer before he was able to walk without falling. Eventually, with Silas's help, he managed a few steps and they began to follow the path again. The fog started to lift and the forest was quiet. The atmosphere had changed completely. All sense of threat had dissipated as though nothing had ever happened.

"When we get out of here, I am going down on my knees to give thanks to the Goddess of Fortune," Martyn vowed as he stumbled along.

"I think we both will," Silas said.

"Goddess, give us a sign to fortify us," Martyn muttered under his breath.

They noticed a dim light up ahead and suddenly found themselves on the very edge of the forest, near a familiar rocky outcrop they both instantly recognised. They let out a cry of delight upon seeing it and started running towards it, whooping and laughing like a couple of children. Remembering their vow, however, they paused, knelt and gave fervent thanks to the Goddess for leading them safely through the danger they had encountered.

Their prayers done, they rose to their feet and, as they did so, they saw the sky beyond and noticed how high the sun had climbed. It looked like it was almost noon. Had they really been in the forest that long?

They headed for the outcrop of rock, knowing that the edge of the forest was just beyond it. As they approached, they heard the sound of water splashing into a pool, which puzzled them. Silas went around the outcrop to investigate and, to his amazement, found a spring where previously there had been simply a bare expanse of rock. He called out to Martyn, who ran over to look.

"This is the sign I asked for," Martyn said seriously. "This spring definitely wasn't here when we walked through with the girls last night."

"Well, whatever it is and however it came to be here, I am just glad that it is," Silas said. "I'm going to have a drink. My head is pounding."

"You never could hold your ale," jeered Martyn, dodging as Silas laughingly aimed a punch at him.

Silas knelt down at the edge of the pool and reached out a cupped hand to catch some of the water. It sparkled, even in the soft green light. He drank eagerly, finding it cold and refreshing. He splashed some on his face and neck, then knelt back on his heels and breathed deeply. All at once, he opened his eyes wide and stared at Martyn.

"My headache has gone," he said incredulously. "Completely gone. I don't even feel tired any more. I feel like I've just had the best night's sleep of my life."

Martyn laughed. "Don't exaggerate," he chuckled, leaning down to catch some water to drink. He swallowed a few handfuls, then gave a satisfied sigh and started to strip off his shoes and socks. "I think I'll just soak my feet for a moment. Bál's Claws, they ache!"

He rolled up his trouser legs, settled himself comfortably and lowered his feet into the water. Almost immediately, his expression changed to one of sheer disbelief and he lifted one foot out of the water to look at it.

"What's the matter?" asked Silas, who was lying down with his hands behind his head, staring up at the leaves.

"My feet," Martyn said hesitantly. "The second I put them in the water, they stopped hurting. That very moment."

Silas leaned up on one elbow. "Now do you believe me?" he asked. "Exactly the same thing happened with my headache."

"This is the work of the Goddess," Martyn declared. He replaced his foot in the pool and leaned forward to catch another handful of water, which he splashed gratefully on his face. "Ah, that's better," he sighed.

The two of them sat for a long while without moving or speaking, completely overawed by their experiences and feeling somehow different within themselves, as though they had undergone a profound change.

"I'm not religious," Silas said suddenly. "You know that. But this spring is obviously sacred and it's been shown to us first. We need to do something. You know, to protect it."

"Something that honours the Goddess," agreed Martyn. "Something important. Significant." He stared thoughtfully at the spring, listening to the soothing sound of its waters. "I never really believed in ghosts, or fairies, or pixies, or any of that sort of thing," he said. "Yet now, I'm not so sure. I don't know what happened last night or where this spring came from, but suddenly I feel a bit bad for laughing at people when they said they had had a supernatural experience. What has happened here is incredible and I'm not sure I know how to deal with it. I think I might go and talk to the Priest of Bál. We both should."

"We need to build a shrine," Silas exclaimed, sitting bolt upright. "Or a temple. There needs to be a place where people can come and pray to the Goddess. Do you think we could do that?"

"Don't see why not," Martyn agreed. "How would we go about it?"

They began throwing ideas around and after a while, their rumbling stomachs sent them heading for home. They passed a couple of friends who had seen them in the inn the previous evening and, assuming that the two had spent the night with the girls, they teased them good-naturedly. Silas and Martyn simply smiled and winked, leaving their friends chuckling.

From that moment, their lives changed entirely. They went to see the Priest of Bál and told him everything that had happened. He was initially suspicious and sceptical, for their reputation preceded them and he thought they were playing a trick on him, but he became immensely excited when they told him about the spring, insisting on hurrying up to the forest to see it for himself. He was an old man with poor sight, so when he asked for a demonstration, Martyn suggested that he bathe his eyes in the water. Silas stared at his friend in concern, for they only had their own experiences to rely upon and he wasn't keen on using someone's eyes to experiment with the spring's powers. Before he could protest, the priest had leaned forward with a cupped hand and splashed some of the water onto his face.

He blinked the water away and the two friends saw his expression change as he looked around him. His jaw dropped and he caught his breath as he looked up at the canopy overhead. "I can see everything!" he gasped. "I can see everything as clearly as if I was a young man! It's a miracle! This truly is the sacred well of the Goddess!"

The three of them began in earnest to spread the word about the well and it wasn't long before pilgrims came from far and wide to see it for themselves. Silas and Martyn built a large shelter around the spring and the pool so they could protect it from anyone who might wish to damage or pollute it. However, they soon found that the water itself carried its own punishment. In the early days, several people helped themselves to some of the water, two or three of their party distracting Silas and Martyn while the rest quickly dipped containers into the pool and hid them under their cloaks. The friends later heard that every single one of them had lost their sight. Some of them had used the water, some had sold it for a vast amount of gold and a couple had not yet decided what to do with it, but whatever course of action they had taken subsequently, each of them woke up one day to discover that they were blind. Those who still had some of the water immediately travelled back to the spring to return it, but it made no difference. The damage had been done.

Of course, this helped Martyn and Silas immensely, as no one was willing to risk their sight and as the story spread throughout the area and on into neighbouring provinces, they found that instances of theft ceased almost overnight. Pilgrims came, paid proper respect to the Goddess, made an offering and a donation to the temple fund and enjoyed the full benefit of the water's healing properties.

Months passed, people came in their hundreds each day, donations were made towards the building of the temple and the townspeople welcomed their visitors with open arms. Silas and Martyn, who had always been well-liked, were now greatly respected, not just because they were the favoured of the Goddess of Fortune, but also because they had brought good luck to each and every person in the town. The influx of pilgrims, who all needed to eat and sleep, meant that the inns had a steady, thriving trade, to the point that one or two of them were eventually able to double in size and employ dozens of townspeople. Skilled craftspeople were attracted to the town, as were merchants and labourers. New shops sprang up, the roads were improved, houses were built and the town enjoyed wealth such as it had never known. The size of the donations began to increase as people gave thanks for the wonderful life they enjoyed and soon, there was enough to begin construction. Martyn and Silas oversaw every aspect and it was not long before the temple was complete – a graceful building of white stone, with the spring, pool and outcrop of rock the focal point in the centre of a large courtyard. There was a shrine to the Goddess at one end and an apartment for the newly-appointed priest beyond. It was not long before a monastery was founded by a new religious order and the Brothers of Clarity have been linked to the Goddess of Fortune ever since.

Silas eventually married and moved from ostling to breeding horses. He had a real talent for spotting a champion, which, coupled with his fame, brought him many customers from all over the Empire and overseas. He made a great deal of money, a sizeable portion of which went straight to the temple. He bought a large house in the town, then built an inn, which became very profitable, so he built another in a town not far away, which also did well. For a while, he and Martyn were the most famous men in the Empire and could hardly set foot out of doors without being petitioned, or stopped by total strangers for a chat. Silas took it all in his stride, but Martyn, to everyone's surprise, reacted very differently.

When the horse breeding enterprise had taken off, Silas invited Martyn to become his business partner, but Martyn had declined. He, too, had seen an increase in custom and was constantly busy, but for some reason, it made him uncomfortable. He did not understand why this should be so, for he had always wanted to expand his business, yet the more successful he became, the more deeply unhappy he found himself. Whenever he could get away, he went up to the temple and began spending more and more time there talking with the priest until, eventually, he announced to Silas one day that he intended to join the Brothers of Clarity. Silas and his family were in the temple to witness Martyn cast off his secular life and become Brother Martinus.

The Temple of the Goddess of Fortune looks today much as it did then. Ancient plans show that the trees encroached on it considerably more than they do now, and a sizeable portion of that part of the forest was cleared some years ago to create an area near the temple where people could leave their carriages. The town, of course, continued to thrive and expand and is said to be one of the best and happiest places to live in the Empire. If you ever visit, make sure you go to the botanical gardens and see the statues of Silas and Brother Martinus at the edge of the lake.

After the temple was built, stories of supernatural occurrences in the forest stopped completely. Nonetheless, if you decide to travel through the forest, make sure you have torches – and if you do hear anything out of the ordinary, turn your jacket inside out, just in case, and trust in fortune.

Bál's Folly

For many generations after orchestrating the death of their brother Frodleikr, his four chromatic siblings still desperately wanted Bál's creatures to hold them in same high esteem Frodleikr had enjoyed. In spite of everything, their natures had not changed in the slightest and they still failed to understand why they were not well-liked. Their metallic siblings Jafnadr and Hreysti gathered many followers who worshipped them, while they themselves could only muster a few supporters. They saw this as a failing of Bál's creatures, however, rather than any fault of their own and thus they continued for decades, growing ever more bitter and resentful. The four of them genuinely believed that they should be worshipped as gods.

It did not help that even in death, Frodleikr remained more popular. Deities such as the Goddess of Fortune and their father, the Great Bál, were hugely popular because of their benevolence and love for those who followed them, but it simply never occurred to any of the four dragons that changing the way they treated others would stand them in good stead with the people they sought to attract. Instead, they bullied and threatened them, stole crops, burned forests and flattened houses with a well-placed thump of their tails. In short, they did everything they could to make the people hate them, and it worked extremely well. Of course, there were some who shared the same resentments and jealousies and these people found a gathering of like minds associated with the four dragons. Admittedly, it was a very small and select gathering, but it gave them a place to vent their own frustrations and anger and they joined the dragons' supporters simply because no other group wanted them. They were a band of misfits seething in their own inner conflict with a vastly inflated sense of their own importance.

Bál saw all this and it troubled him deeply. He had always hoped that his children would emulate their mother, the lost Máni, who had had the sweetest, most caring nature of any living creature. Jafnadr and Hreysti honoured their mother daily, yet their siblings seemed to have forgotten her very existence. Bál summoned them periodically to remind them of their duty to their mother, but no matter how many times he spoke with them, the words glanced off their scales as though they were the blows of a toy sword. Nothing changed.

Eventually Bál's temper was strained to breaking point. He arranged to meet with his children in a distant valley in the heart of the Hheserakhian desert, then, when they were assembled and awaiting him, sent a great flood in order to sweep away their evil and try to save the souls of those who supported and followed their wicked ways. It had not worked. The four of them had managed to save themselves, clinging to the sides of the ravine as the flood waters gushed and churned beneath them. Needless to say, this made relations with their father and siblings even more strained and uncomfortable.

Hefnd, who held the strongest conviction that she should be a deity, managed on one occasion to wheedle her way into the royal court in Qalarmah, one of the lands to the east of the Hheserakhian Empire, with which the Empire had a mutually beneficial and profitable trade agreement of long standing. She claimed that the Empire was setting plans in motion to cheat Qalarmah and made up a number of tall tales to give her claim a semblance of truth. The King, however, was no fool. When Hefnd was elsewhere in the palace, he summoned his envoys, who were recently returned from Hheserakh.

"Tell me," he said, as the three of them bowed low before him, "when you were at the Imperial Palace, was there any indication of unrest between our nations, or a suggestion that the terms of our Treaty should be changed?"

The envoys exchanged puzzled glances before assuring the King that they had been welcomed with as much warmth and ceremony as they usually were. The Emperor had arranged sumptuous banquets in their honour, there was non-stop entertainment every evening after the day's business was concluded and there had been a significant amount of talk about increasing the products the Empire exported. There had been nothing negative whatsoever about any aspect of their time at the Imperial Court.

The King thanked them for their service and duty and dismissed them. He then went to his office and wrote a letter to the Emperor, advising him what he had been told and asking if the Emperor was aware that such claims were being made. He took the letter to one of his wizards so it could be sent by an animal messenger, as he was understandably impatient for a reply.

The reply came by animal messenger even more swiftly than he had dared hope. The Emperor thanked him for his care and expressed alarm at the claims, for he was in the midst of drawing up a proposal for the King to consider which would expand trade for both of them. He assured the King that, contrary to what he was being told, there was no ill-will towards Qalarmah from Hheserakh and the King should take whatever steps he felt necessary to quell the lies.

It had only been a matter of some five or six days since the King had sent his letter, but in that time, Hefnd had been busy. Many in the kingdom had never seen a living dragon and what they knew of them came from books. Therefore, the chance to see and even talk to one meant that Hefnd was enjoying the popularity she so desperately craved. She was good at weaving words and before long, had gathered a sizeable group of followers, but, true to form, she very quickly overstepped herself by urging the people of Qalarmah to wage war on Hheserakh. The Qalarmians started to become suspicious, especially merchants and other travellers who had strong connections with the Empire. They were unwilling to proceed when the only evidence anyone had of their trade partner's alleged wrongdoing was the word of a dragon with a poor reputation amongst every race alive – and a few undead. Once the King had heard back from the Emperor, he issued a Royal Proclamation to announce that he would shortly be entering into discussion with the Emperor about ways in which they could build their trade relationship even further. The people then knew they had been fooled and Hefnd suddenly found that she was no longer welcome.

The Emperor seethed with anger as he penned his response to the King. He stomped along the corridors in the Imperial Palace to deliver the missive to his wizards in person, then stomped back to his council chamber and summoned the council. He told them what had happened and that something had to be done about Hefnd.

The discussion did not go well. Two of the older members of the council suggested that Hefnd was actually working in their best interests, for the trade agreement favoured Qalarmah rather than Hheserakh and if there was war, Hheserakh would easily overpower Qalarmah and could then take whatever goods it wanted without the need for a treaty.

The rest of the council was horrified and one counsellor went so far as to say that they were both were out-of-touch dinosaurs still rattling on about ancient grudges between the two lands which had long since been put aside, and that neither of them had any right to hold such esteemed positions if they were going to openly spout such treason. The meeting had degenerated rapidly and the Emperor had broken it up, sanctioned several counsellors for various misdemeanours, then headed to his library to see if his books would yield the wisdom he sought. He sat up most of the night, leafing through tome after tome, yet found nothing of use. The following day, after a sleepless night, he sought the counsel of his priests, but they had no idea how to deal with a creature such as Hefnd, especially since she had three siblings who were just as problematic as she was. Remove one problem, the priests warned, and another would pop up in its place.

In the end, the priests advised the Emperor to petition the Great Bál himself and pray for guidance at his temple in the Imperial City.

The Emperor put together an extremely generous offering and went to the Temple of the Great Bál, which was in the centre of the Imperial City, not far from the Palace. It stood along one side of a huge square plaza and was an impressive sight, for it was four storeys high and worshippers had to climb a flight of twenty-one stone steps to reach it. There were seven white marble pillars along the frontage and at the pinnacle of the cornice above, a huge golden disc representing Bál's fire.

The Emperor made his offering and went to the shrine of the Great Bál to pray. He remained in the temple for most of the day, praying and meditating, then returned to the palace as the sun was setting, certain that he had heard the voice of Bál.

The Great Bál had indeed heard the Emperor and had immediately gone in search of his wayward offspring, disguised as a tall, dark-skinned man so that he could walk amongst his creatures undetected. As he travelled, he spoke with many people of all races and was deeply disturbed and saddened by what he learned and saw. The more he learned, the more his rage took over. At first, in his anger, he resolved to summon the four of them and destroy them, then bury them in a deep gorge and flood it, so their miserable bones would be lost for all eternity.

However, having sent word to them, he found that he could not bring himself to destroy his own children. He wrestled with his conscience as he waited for them to arrive, distracted by a religious group not far away who had gathered to worship Máni. He paused in his thoughts to listen to their beautiful singing and became lost in the rhythm of their chants, finding himself reliving the song he and Máni had sung to each other. At that moment, he knew that he could not kill his children. Instead, he decided that he should first try to reason with them and help them understand the ways in which they differed from their brother and sister.

One by one the four of them arrived at the appointed place. Bál had chosen to remain in his disguise, but each of the younger dragons knew that it was he.

Bál tried. He used every ounce of persuasion he possessed, but his children simply scoffed at him and ridiculed his efforts. No matter how reasonable he was, no matter how helpful and gentle, they rebuffed every attempt he made to show them how to gain what they so desired.

Eventually, even Bál's almost limitless patience wore out. He roared at them, demanding to know why they enjoyed creating discord and war between his creatures. Hefnd replied shortly that they wanted to be worshipped as gods and the creatures had to be shown that it was their duty to do so.

Bál was furious. He shed his disguise, almost blinding them with his divine radiance. He could feel his anger as a physical presence, coursing through his body and making his obsidian scales ripple. "You want to be worshipped as gods?" he thundered. "Your behaviour is unbecoming of a deity! You are not worthy of such an honour. You do not even take the time to respect the memory of your beloved mother. I am not surprised that no one has built a temple in your name – not one of you deserves it."

As he spoke, he gestured with one huge hand and a ball of dark energy swirled into existence in his palm. "I curse each one of you to an eternal half-life, beloved of no one, worshipped by no one, thought of by no one and remembered by no one. Your lives and fates will be forever inextricably entwined. From this moment on, you are no longer my blood, my offspring. You are the Amáttr, the despicable, and I curse you!"

So saying, he hurled the ball of dark energy, which transformed mid-air into a huge thunderbolt which hurtled towards the four dragons and hit them full force. The air rippled wildly with the impact of the blow and the ground rumbled as dozens of earthquakes were set off around the world. The skies darkened and clouded Bál's fire as the father unleashed the full power of his pent-up fury on his children. A vast dust cloud billowed out, swamping the area with its choking, cloying, swirling particles. The sound of the thunderbolt was so loud that it was heard around the world and reverberating in the air for many minutes afterwards.

Silence fell. The dust cloud began to thin and settle. Bál kept his eyes fixed on the spot where the thunderbolt had hit. For there was something there, something moving. Something that screamed and roared as it clawed its way out of the crater the thunderbolt had left behind.

It had the body of a dragon, although horribly twisted and misshapen, and there was not one but five heads, each staring in loathing and fury at their father. The thing staggered as it heaved itself out of the crater, as though each of the five heads had its own idea about which direction it should take. The five faces were contorted in agony as it struggled to understand what had happened to it.

Bál watched without pity or mercy.

"Never again will you be able to hurt anyone with your evil, self-serving ways!" he snapped. "Your misshapen form is henceforth your prison and you shall, forever more, suffer the pains and agonies of all those whom you have wronged throughout your wicked lives, especially your brother Frodleikr. I banish you to a half-life underground, where my creatures will be safe from your vile machinations and cruelty!"

With that, he hurled another thunderbolt and the ground beneath the creature cracked and split open with another terrifying boom that was heard the world over.

Jafnadr and Hreysti heard it also and knew instantly that it did not bode well. They immediately went in search of their father and found him staring down into a vast void at a creature the likes of which they had never before laid eyes upon.

"Father," whispered Hreysti, "what have you done?"

In response, Bál unleashed another thunderbolt and the two metallic siblings clung to each other in fear as he hurled it. The sides of the fissure in the earth began to crumble and cave in, sending an avalanche of rocks and rubble cascading down its slopes, burying the foul creature below. A furious, tortured, agonised scream rent the air and then all was silent.

Bál turned and flew away without another word, leaving Jafnadr and Hreysti to work out what had occurred. They feared that their father's anger had gone too far and that he had shown an unforgiveable lack of control, but they had no power to undo what he had done. They sat silently by the ruined land until some of Bál's creatures started appearing, nervously searching for the source of the terrible noises they had heard from many miles away. The two dragons bade the people to spread the news that their four wicked siblings were no more.

They did not say that a new evil slumbered in the depths of the earth, for they sincerely hoped that it would remain there forever and that none of Bál's creatures would ever discover it.

Time passed and, every now and then, stories would surface about a five-headed dragon. Some claimed to have seen it. Some said that they had heard its terrible wings as it flew overhead late at night. It was seen in caverns, catacombs, near burial grounds and at old battle sites, especially those where there had been a significant loss of life. Some had heard its voice, a terrible harsh, ragged snarl. Its words, such as had been overheard, were the mutterings of a damaged mind. Occasionally, particularly in places where there were clusters of sightings, the word "Tiamat" was discovered, crudely scratched into the ground or on the side of a building as though with a huge claw. Over time, the word became associated with the creature and was eventually used as its name. Many decades later, the first Cult of Tiamat arose and Jafnadr and Hreysti despaired, for in trying to remove one evil from the world their father had created something far worse.

Although there are numerous recorded sightings of a five-headed dragon, particularly amongst those belonging to its cult, the beast has never approached or interacted with any of Bál's creatures. It simply slinks from shadow to shadow, watching, but never a part of the world. In areas where there are many cave systems, loud screams of agony are sometimes heard, screams so dreadful that the very air throbs as it carries them. It is said that this is the cry of Tiamat as it voices its terrible plight so the world can hear and remember.

Many believe that Tiamat is waiting for the arrival of one powerful enough to break its father's curse and once again restore it to full life. That is certainly what its cultists fervently hope for.

Yet who could ever be powerful enough to break the curse of the Great Bál himself?

Lightning Source UK Ltd.
Milton Keynes UK
UKHW02f1853100818
327074UK00003B/11/P

9 781999 755416